Dedication

For my family.
You all know who you are.

"Be where you are, otherwise you will miss your life." Buddha

EMILY: Does anyone ever realize life while they live it...every, every minute?

STAGE MANAGER: No. Saints and poets maybe...they do some.

—Thornton Wilder, <u>Our Town</u>

Happenstance

Debra Loughead

Print ISBNs
Amazon Print 9780228632696
Ingram Spark 9780228632702
BWL Print 9780228632719
B&N Print 9780228632726

BWL Publishing Inc.

*Books we love to write …
Authors around the world.*

http://bwlpublishing.ca

Eight Years Ago — Tara

"Mommy, where are we going? Can you tell me again?"

"I just told you Tara honey, we're going on a little holiday. Only for a while."

"And why can't Daddy come with us?"

"I already told you that, too. Like three times already. He's very busy. He has to work. He can't come on this holiday. And besides, it's a special getaway only for mothers and their children."

"Will we be going on another holiday with my dad sometime soon? Like that time we went camping last summer and he pushed you down and you hurt your wrist. And it was an accident. Remember Mom?"

"Yes, I remember that very well Tara Bear. The one and only time we ever tried camping. I'm not sure we'll ever be doing that again. It didn't work out very well at all, did it?"

"So anyway, what's it like there, where we're going. And why do we have to take the bus. I'm hot. And my backpack is making me even sweatier. And the lady beside me has bad breath."

"Shhh. Tara not so loud. We're taking the bus because Daddy doesn't know we're going. It'll be a big surprise for him. Sometimes daddies need to have a holiday from their families. And guess what? There's lots of moms like me and kids like you where were going. It's called Helena's Haven. We might have to share a room with some other people. They'll have toys and books for you to play with. And food and snacks. You'll like it there, you'll see."

"And will you miss Daddy while we're staying there? Will you?"

"Um...I'm not sure what to say about..."

"I won't miss him, Mom. I plug my ears whenever he yells at us, and you yell back. And I don't like it when he pushes you against the wall and says mean things. I always close my eyes."

"I know, honey. I know. That's why we need a little break right now. Here. Play with my phone for a bit. We'll be there soon."

Eight years ago—Sophie

"What's wrong with Mom, Dhanu? Why won't she stop crying?"

"She's sad, Sophie, she's oh so very sad, poor thing. Come, sit here beside me."

"But why is she so sad? Why is she always staying in bed and crying? And never eating the food that you take up to the bedroom for her?"

"Because she's a bit sick too, my dear. It's called 'depression', the way she's feeling now. She's stuck in a place that she can't get out of."

"I think Jonah is stuck there too, and he's scared. Every time he looks at Mom he starts crying. And he comes into my room at night and asks me what's happening. But I don't know. He hears Mom and Dad arguing in their room at night, like I do."

"I'm sure he's scared, Sophie. Your parents are going through something right now. But it will all turn out okay. Just wait and see. And try to be patient. She will feel better soon, I'm sure."

"Is that why Daddy's taking her to the hospital right now? Because she can't stop crying and she won't try to eat all her favourite food? Even macaroni and cheese and chocolate cake?"

"That's right, my dear. It's been going on for too long now. She needs help from doctors".

"But when will she come back? I'll miss her. At least you'll be here though. I love that you came to live with us last year. I hope you stay forever. I love that you're always here when Mom and Dad aren't. It's like you're another mother for us, right?"

"I like to think of myself as your sister friend, Sophie. You can only really ever have one true mother who loves you more than anything else in the world".

"I like that, Dhanu. We can be sister friends forever. I really hope Mom feels better soon though".

"Me too, sister friend. Me too. That's why I gave her my special moonstone ring to wear until she starts to feel better. For good luck and strength. It's my most prized possession, you know."

Table of Contents

Chapter One 11

Chapter Two 35

Chapter Three................................... 60

Chapter Four 83

Chapter Five 112

Chapter Seven 157

Chapter Eight 182

Chapter Nine 208

Chapter Ten................................. 231

Chapter Eleven 254

Chapter One

Tara

Pretending to be someone else for a while has its benefits. When you're in an acting role, you get to live in a completely different world, in someone else's skin. You can forget about your own issues and focus on your character's problems. But I've had so much on my mind lately, that I just can't get excited about my friend Priya's newfound happiness over trying it for the first time.

"I am so pumped for this, Tara. I didn't think I'd ever be in a play!" Priya says.

"I promised you'd love it," I tell her. "Now do you finally believe me?"

On Thursday as we're heading home from a rehearsal after school, I fake listening as Priya rambles on about being a cast member in the upcoming school production of *Our Town*. This is her very first play ever, and she's totally caught up in the thrill of being on stage. Since I've been in a couple of school play productions in the past, I know that feeling all too well.

Warm April sunshine beats down on my head as I kick a random stone along in front of me. As usual, I'm not in a hurry to get home. I can never be sure which version of my mom will be waiting to greet me. The hopeful mom, chirping as she clatters around the kitchen fixing dinner? Or the one with sadness in her eyes, sitting at the table scratching lottery tickets, or the chipped polish off her fingernails.

Lost in negative thoughts, I watch the stone tumble along in front of me. It sort of feels like my life right now, just bumping along and not getting anywhere worthwhile. But when it rolls to a stop, my sparkle radar is on high alert. A shard of sunshine reflects off something glittery at just the right angle. A sudden flash and my eyes are instantly drawn to that gleam. I bend down to pick it up, and suck in my breath.

"Wow," I whisper. "Check this out, Priya. It's amazing!"

Beside me Priya lets out a soft whistle of surprise.

We both lean in for a closer look at the ring nestled in my palm. The stone shimmers like a pale oval moon in its silver setting. And on each shoulder, what looks to be a tiny diamond twinkles like starlight. To me it looks super expensive, but then again, I don't know much about expensive things.

But seriously, how can anyone possibly be so careless.

"Oh my God, is that for real? It looks too nice to be fake," Priya says.

"Come on, it can't possibly be real. What clueless fool would ever lose something as lovely as this, whether it's for real or not, though, right?"

I inspect it closely, turn it over and over in my hand, instantly transfixed by the pearly opalescence of the stone. So gorgeous, so irresistible. Then I do it. Slip the ring on my finger and hold it up in the sunshine. It fits me perfectly. I can't even imagine the possibility of ever owning something so lovely. This shiny thing already makes me feel like a completely different person.

Then for some reason I look over my shoulder, to see if anyone's watching. The street is mostly deserted, except for a bus that just made a drop-off, and someone in the distance, running away fast. When I look back at Priya, she's staring at me with her head tilted, as if she might be thinking things that I don't want to hear. It almost feels like she's judging me for something I haven't even done.

"What are you looking for, Tara?" she says.

What am I looking for? What am I even thinking? Things that I'm not very proud of but can't ignore. Mainly that I want to keep the ring and wonder if anybody else saw me pick it up.

"Well duh," I tell her. "Whoever dropped it, of course. What else would I be thinking?"

"Maybe it was her." Priya points to the figure too far off now to even see distinctly. "That person in the school blazer who just got off the bus. Come on. Let's try and catch up to ask them."

"Catch up?" Hmm. Lately my life is such a colossal disappointment, so un-sparkly. I'm not sure I'm ready to give up the ring just yet. Even the look of it on my finger makes my life seem just a little more glittery. "Oh, too bad. Looks like it's too late already."

Sure enough, the figure is fading into the distance. And then it's hard to tell whether they turned a corner or disappeared into one of the identical brick bungalows that skirt the street. Or vanished into thin air. Someone magical, leaving me a gift to find? Hah. How I wish.

"Guess I'll just have to keep it now, huh?" I offer a wobbly grin.

"Hah, yeah right," Priya says. "So, will you be taking it to the police station? Or maybe you could stick a sign on a lamppost like people do when they lose their pets?"

Priya expects me to do the right thing. Because I always do the right thing. All my life, for my mom's sake, since she has enough to deal with as it is. But maybe today can be different for a change. Maybe today, there are more possibilities, and maybe I can make a different choice, instead of being so predictable and always making the right one.

Why does every single thing always have to be so hard to figure out? Why can't I ever make a split second decision? *Why?*

"Seriously, I bet it came out of a Cracker Jack box or a claw machine," I say, avoiding an answer about the sign. But when I hold it up to the sunlight again, I know I'm wrong. The way the sun sparkles on the facets of the stones makes it obvious. Clearly this ring isn't a fake.

"Let's see it," Priya says. "My mom inherited lots of expensive old family jewelry."

Reluctantly I slip it off and drop it into her hand. And I watch almost protectively as she turns it over and over to examine it up close. Because I already feel as if it belongs to me and I don't want to part with it.

"Look, it's 18 karat gold." She points out an etching on the inside of the band. "It says so on the hallmark."

"Except that it's silver, Pri," I remind her.

"White gold looks silver. I can tell this is expensive. And for sure that's a moonstone. Which comes from the same place that my family originates, in Sri Lanka. Those are diamonds, on the shoulders. Nothing twinkles the way diamonds do."

"Wow I wish I owned a ring like this. But clearly that will never happen."

"Well, I've heard that if you turn something in at the police station and nobody claims it, then eventually you get it back. That's what I'd do, if I were you." Priya smiles as she drops the ring into my hand.

"Hmm, that's a good plan," I say, then wrinkle my nose. "Maybe I'll just wear it for tonight, then turn it in to the police tomorrow. Or maybe I'll put up some signs. Not sure yet. Gosh I seriously can't stop looking at it." I hold it up to the sunlight again, still transfixed.

Priya is frowning a bit. I'm not sure I like the way she's looking at me, all judgy or something. "You're not thinking 'finders keepers', right?"

Losers weepers. I frown back at her. "What kind of person do you think I am anyway?" I ask, forcing a grin as I slip the ring back on. "Anyway, right now my finger really is the safest place for this awesome ring, right? Seeya tomorrow."

I head in one direction and Priya heads in the other. And I stare at that ring, watch it glimmer in the sunshine all the way home. I so wish it could be mine instead of someone else's. So I could have it just to stare at whenever I want to cheer myself up. Because the sad fact is, I'm in desperate need of a sparkly makeover. If not a physical one, then for sure a mental one.

Over the past year, my mom has been trying hard to make our lives better after difficult times. She actually found the courage to kick my lame dad out of our lives forever. We were so sick and tired of his cruel yelling and bullying. I begged her to stay strong and make a move.

So, I was thrilled when she finally told him to leave so that the two of us could get on with a new chapter of our lives, and not have to worry anymore about what he might say or do next. He was always so unpredictable, it felt like we were constantly living on the edge. We hardly ever hear from him now, thankfully. But somehow it feels as if our lives still lack sparkle. One dreary day just seems to melt into the next. Nothing ever changes. Mom seems to be stuck in a brand new rut now too, and not trying hard enough to climb out and to actually get herself a life.

Most days, living with my mom, Marie Kowalchuk, who ditched her married last name, feels a bit like riding an upside down rollercoaster. Constantly bounced and jolted and jiggled, never knowing what sort of rush is around the next corner, depending on how her day went. She's always had high hopes of becoming a certified esthetician and someday opening her own in-home salon. But that never took off, so she started applying for salon jobs instead.

The problem is, whenever she lands a job at a new salon, she leaves within a few days or weeks. She has all sorts of good excuses. Usually though, it's because she disapproves of the lack of quality, the poor sanitary conditions. I admire her for her ethical stand but have a feeling she might be settling back into her gloomy blue funk, now that she's adjusted to Dad being gone. The truth is, I'm sick of living on social assistance and always rolling coins to take to the bank. Sometimes I feel guilty for thinking she doesn't try hard enough. But what could our lives be like if Mom worked even harder to make things better for us? I have my doubts that will ever happen though. She doesn't seem to have the confidence she'd need to pull it off.

Just before stepping inside, I slip the ring off and hold it tight inside my fist. Nope, I'm not quite ready to part with it, because I'm not finished looking at it yet. I plan on holding it under my bedroom desk lamp to examine it even more closely. And to search online to find out everything I can about moonstones, and exactly how much a ring like this could be worth. Not that it matters much, since I'm turning it in. Eventually, anyway.

Silence greets me as I step through the front door of our townhouse. Mom promised she was going to the employment office to check out the job listings today. But she should have been home long ago. My heart lifts. Maybe she got herself a job straight off. Maybe she's actually employed again and won't be moping around the house feeling sorry for herself. Maybe I can stop worrying about her so much and focus more on myself for a change.

In the kitchen, I spot the note on the table. When I sit down to read it, my heart goes into a tailspin. *Gone to the coffee shop. Back in a while. xoxo*

I know exactly what that means. She's meeting up with another guy. Somehow my mom believes that she needs a man in her life to feel fulfilled. I can't figure out why. We've barely recovered from being mistreated by my dad. I still shudder at the thought of how we needed help from a shelter once. An unforgettable nightmare you'd never dream could happen to you. But the counselors there were kind to us. At least there was that.

So how can my mom possibly begin to trust someone else when she hasn't even healed completely yet, and might never? Every single time she goes out to meet with someone she found on an online dating site, she leaves the house put together and smiling. And she inevitably comes home in a glum mood, with tear-streaked mascara.

Why does she keep on doing this to herself? And to me?

I slip the ring back on and throw a ham and cheese sandwich together for dinner. Then I sit at the table looking over my lines for the *Our Town* script, a prize-winning American play by Thornton Wilder. Personally, I think it's the most depressing play ever, since in Act III pretty much everyone is dead. I didn't get the main role that I wanted, 'Emily Webb', which an older student named Iris nailed, of course.

There was no point in Priya and me auditioning for the plum main roles anyway. The best parts went to the more experienced cast members. But the coolest surprise came when I was chosen as understudy for Emily because I'd been in plays before. What a thrill! It means learning a ton of lines and showing up at every rehearsal, but I'm okay with that. Memorizing lines gives me something to focus on, lets me turn into someone else for a while and forget about my drag of a life that's weighing me down. And even though the possibility of having to step in for Iris gives me the jitters, it's an honour to even be chosen.

The ring keeps catching my eye as I run over the 'Emily Webb' lines. I already know the part so well, that during rehearsals I whisper the lines along with Iris. Iris gets to act opposite Silas Symonds, who plays the role of her boyfriend/husband, 'George Gibbs'.

Silas, who's a senior, is everyone's crush ever since he showed up partway through the school year. He'd never look twice at a girl my age though, especially one with mousy brown curls like mine, green eyes too far apart and a too-small nose. Plus, he could have his pick of any girl in drama. Still, being near him makes me feel all fluttery from the inside out, as if I've swallowed a flock of butterflies. We all secretly swoon over Silas.

When I hear the key in the front door, I slip the ring off again and tuck it into the pocket of my jeans. Pat it like it's a lucky charm or something. Mom shuffles along the hallway. I wait, wincing, to see her regretful face. But when she reaches the kitchen, my eyebrows fly up. She's actually smiling for real.

"Score!" she says. Then she walks over to the table and gives me a hefty hug.

"You found a job today?" I ask with hope in my voice.

"Oh God no, Tara," she says. "But I think this new fella could be a keeper."

New fella? Really, a new man in her life? That's the last thing I need to hear. Isn't our life complicated enough already? Does she really need another man around to send her heart soaring until he eventually breaks it? She never thinks things through, and I wish I could just tell her to forget about this ridiculous need for a guy, but she won't listen to reasoning when her head is in the clouds. Ugh, it makes me want to scream. But instead, I force a flimsy smile.

"That's nice, I guess, Mom." I push back my chair, stand up and head for my room. "Hope this one works out for once. I mean, you haven't ever had the best luck with men, have you?"

Long pause. "But I've met him quite a few times now, you know. And it's going really well," she calls behind me in a fake-chirpy voice. "Don't you want to know more about him? Even just his name?" I can sense her disappointment, but I resist turning around.

"Maybe later. I've got tons of homework," I lie, then get out of there fast. And plan on avoiding her for the rest of the evening. She'll just be buried on cyber dating sites anyway, for when this one inevitably doesn't work out, since she's joined a few of them. It makes me sick to see her slouched in front of the computer clicking on faces she's attracted to, swiping right again and again. How many of them are phonies? Too many, for sure. I just don't trust my easily duped Mom.

She fell for Dad, after all.

* * *

Sophie

When I blow through the front door at high speed after school on Thursday, I'm already in a bad mood. Why is it that nothing ever works out the way your mind tricks you into believing it might? As I was rushing home from the bus stop, I could see it all playing out in my too-busy brain. The welcoming look on his heart-stopping face when he spotted me coming up the driveway, all out of breath, with my long wind-ruffled hair, his eager smile, at long last the invitation to...

"Honey have you seen my ring from Dhanu? I can't find it anywhere."

My mom is standing on the staircase in one of her loose caftans, a headscarf draped over her enviable thick and wavy ash blond hair. She looks like some retro hippy. Always trying to put on a show, too. So pathetically dramatic. The last thing I need to interrupt my self-pity party right now is another confrontation with Mom.

"Mom, how many times are you going to ask me the same question. I told you I haven't got a clue where your ring is. Why are you so obsessed with that stupid thing anyway?"

"Because it has special meaning for me," she explains yet again, with an odd far-off look in her eyes. She makes a grand sweeping gesture at the ceiling and her bangle bracelets rattle. "It reminds me of Dhanu. And of everything that used to be so beautiful so very long ago."

So very long ago? Dhanu just barely left. Her bed's probably still warm. What's it been? Less than a month?

"You need to try and get over it," I snap at my mom, a bit too harshly, and her face drops. "You're always acting so dramatic. You're not in university drama anymore, right?"

"Sophie, it's not just some cheap bauble, you know. I really need to find it. She gave it to me in trust before she left. And you know what she said about the properties of a moonstone."

"Oh come on, Mom, really? The ring will turn up eventually. You're always losing stuff and finding it. So, I'm begging you, don't ask me about it again. I'm so sick of that ring!"

I walk right past her stunned face, up the spiral staircase, and along the too-slippery hardwood to my bedroom and slam the door a little too hard. I fling my navy school blazer on the floor; let my grey school slacks drop in a puddle around my ankles and kick them across the room. Then I pull on my favourite worn sweatpants and a t-shirt. I lay down on my bed, stare up at the ceiling; wonder what to do next.

That's the first thing Mom has to say to me when I walk in after school? Not 'how was your day', or 'how was your math test', or 'how is your relationship with ______ going'. Because all she cares about is that stupid ring. Ever since she put it on her finger, I swear she's started actually believing that her life is on some new fast track to happiness. And she's been totally fixated with the idea of it ever since. Always trying to point out dumb coincidences that don't even make any sense. Like finding a pair of 'really groovy' shoes online in her size and shade. Last pair! Wow, it must be because of the ring! And trying to convince Jonah and me that something mysterious is happening and our lives are changing, getting better. 'You'll see,' she keeps on telling us. 'This ring symbolizes a whole new start for our family now, kids.'

Wrong, Mom. Even though the internet would have you believe it's true. You can find just about anything you'd like to believe online, though. That's how it works. A vast chasm of misinformation that too many gullible people easily fall for. Almost every day, I wonder about how I've gotten so bitter that I even have to think that way. Then I think back on my life so far, and figure it out pretty fast.

To anyone on the outside, it would seem as if our family leads a charmed life. Our dad is vice president of a bank and has to fly all over the world too many times every year. Mom gets to accompany him now and then. But she's mostly been stuck at home with us, finding new ways to waste all our dad's money. Over the years she's consulted with colour technicians to help pick the hues that suit her skin tone the best. She's had her aura read and had a homeopath help guide her holistically. She's been going to yoga classes for ages, and to some sort of salt caves. Seriously what a waste. If there's a way to spend money on useless things, our mother will find a way to do it. Although we truly do have epic winter vacations in Turks and Caicos.

Back when we were younger, my brother and I, Mom managed to squeeze a live-in nanny/housekeeper out of Dad. Guilted him into getting one because she was stuck alone so often and needed help. Hence Dhanu, who was more a mom to us than our own. And ever since she went back to her homeland last month, we've been mostly stuck alone with Mom. And a weekly cleaning service that doesn't provide meals for us every day like good old Dhanu did, cooking up fabulous Instagram-worthy plates of food for us every single day. Jonah and I are missing her like crazy, because she's been everything to us that our mother never was.

The other great thing about Dhanu was that she became my closest confidante through middle school, and even in my first years of high school. She knew every single crush that I had and always came up with great advice to get me through heartbreaks. She helped me with my math homework because I suck so bad. She helped me out when I got my period for the first time way too young. And she was a shoulder to cry on when Mom was falling apart eight years back, distant, distracted and unavailable, self-medicating with wine in her bedroom when she didn't have an appointment outside of the house. Knocking herself out at night with the benzos her doctor prescribed when she complained of sleeping poorly because of anxiety. That was up until antidepressants were prescribed to her after she crashed and are apparently keeping her in some sort of remission, which I highly doubt.

Before heading back to Sri Lanka to become a personal support worker for her ailing mother, Dhanu gave the moonstone ring to my mom, who has always been enthralled with its misty opalescence. She told Mom those milky gemstones that got their name for a reason, possess certain mystical properties. And bestow good fortune upon the wearer. And my mom actually fell for it. But by then she already had a nasty habit of falling for all the wrong things most of the time anyway.

I think I know what's making her so anxious, but I don't dare mention it in case she goes off the deep end. Maybe her magical thinking is helping her deal with that dark cloud of anxiety that always hangs over her head and ours due to past family, well, 'turmoil', I guess you could call it. Or strife, or upheaval, or just complete and utter family shambles. So, because of mom's lurking issues, Dhanu became the person who was always there for me. And I took complete advantage of her attentive ears and comforting arms.

Every time I pass her deserted bedroom now, my heart sinks. Door wide open. Empty drawers and stripped bed. Nothing left of Dhanu but her memory and maybe the odd whiff of her clean flowery smell. Sometimes I even bury my face in the pillows she once slept on just to catch that scent still trapped inside. It's becoming fainter now. She still gets in touch with me now and then by email, but never by phone. Sri Lanka is way too far for that ever to work. No texting like in the old days when I texted her all the time, even when we were under the same roof. With limited internet in their village, she's practically gone back in time. But she has to be there for her mom, who has always been there for her, unlike another mother that I know too well.

"Jonah, did you come across that ring Dhanu gave me," I hear our mother calling up the stairs. "I can't find it anywhere. I'm sure I left it on the dresser. Or maybe it was on my bathroom counter and fell down the drain accidentally? Where is it? Jonah?"

Then I hear an unmuffled groan from my brother's room. The sound of frustration.

"No Mom, and please stop asking me. I haven't seen it, *okay*?"

Then the sound of his door opening and socks sliding along the hardwood floor. A soft knock on my door before it opens a crack.

"What is her problem? Why is she so obsessed with that stupid ring?"

"Did you hear me say come in? Because I don't think I invited you into my room. I mean, can't a girl have a little privacy from her lil brother?"

Jonah just gives me his usual lopsided grin, which always melts me a little. For a younger brother, he isn't really a gigantic knob. The two of us have been sticking together over the years because we have to. Living with parents like ours is a challenge even though it might look like a breeze from people outside our circle. But they have no idea whatsoever.

"So, what's with the ring obsession anyway? Is Mom starting to lose it again or what?"

As hard as he tries, Jonah has a tough time disguising his own anxieties. He's always been a nervous and timid kid but tries to put on a brave face. He's never done well in team sports at our private school, preferring the swim team, as well as chess club this year in grade ten, so relieved that he never has to rely on anyone but himself.

Honestly, sometimes I want to just wrap him up protectively in my arms and tell him to stop worrying so much about absolutely every little thing. Right now, I feel him begging for an answer with his sad green eyes. God, does he ever remind me of our mother. I pat the bed beside me, and he comes over to sit down. Same gesture Dhanu always used on me. I miss her.

"Look Jonah, Mom has issues. We both know that. She always tries to avoid the big ones by focusing on the silly small ones though. It's sort of her coping mechanism, I figure. Right now, she's fixated on that ring because she wants to believe that it has some sort of special power. Which we both know is not even possible. That way she can distract herself from dealing with her distress about how everything has so suddenly changed in our lives. But guess what. I did her a favour. And you have to promise to keep your mouth shut."

"What did you do?" My sad sack brother suddenly perks right up. "Tell me!"

"Hang on, and I'll show you. You have to promise to keep quiet though, okay?"

"Okay, okay, I promise."

"Cross your heart?" I love bugging my brother.

"Come on, seriously! What. Did. You. Do? Just tell me!" He's practically squirming.

"Okay, I will! Right now! Don't breathe a word though. Right?"

He flicks me the middle finger and I laugh, happy that he seems a little distracted right now, a bit less stressed since I've given him something else to think about. Then I dance my way across the room and snatch up my school blazer.

"Check this out." I stuff my hand into the left pocket and dig around. "Oops wrong one. Hang on." For some reason my heart rate picks up. I reach into the other pocket. Empty too. "Crap," I say to Jonah. "Crappety crap."

"What Sophie? Just tell me what you did, will you?"

"It's gone." I groan. "How can it be gone?"

"What's gone?" Jonah looks more stressed out now. Ugh. That wasn't part of my plan.

"The moonstone ring. I found it in the bathroom two mornings ago and tried it on for fun. And left it on. And wore it at school the last couple of days. Trust me, it doesn't work. And she didn't even mention it until this morning."

"Oh no, poor Mom! And why would you even do that?" He is always her biggest defender. "Were you hoping some luck might rub off, and the basketball god next door might magically notice you when he's out in his driveway shooting hoops? Even though he never has?"

"Ouch," I yelp, while trying to erase the image of our gorgeous athletic neighbour in his driveway, jeans and a snug white t-shirt, ropey arms glistening with sweat. Sigh. "Okay, so it's a work in progress. Baby steps, waves and smiles. And I guess I took that stupid ring because I wanted to distract Mom, or something. Make her stew about something else, instead of missing Dhanu so much. I was going to give it back, you know. Come on, help me look for it."

I crawl around my cluttered floor, and my brother joins me. Frantically digging through my strewn stuff in case it fell from my pocket when I tossed my jacket. But nope, no such luck. I sit in the middle of my room feeling a bit dizzy and way too hot, my armpits prickling. Where is that damn ring?

"How could I have lost it on the way home? Wait!" I snap my fingers. "I was running for a bit. Trying to get home faster for some reason which I can't even remember now."

Oh yes, I most certainly can. Because yesterday at the exact same time, he was out in his driveway shooting hoops in all his long, lean and sweaty glory. Not today though, which is why I'd walked in crabby and snapped at Mom in the first place.

"You have to find it for her," Jonah says. "Before she gets depressed and crashes or something. You have to go back. Retrace your steps." He stands up and glares down at me. How has he gotten so tall so fast? Eighteen months younger than me and he's already passed me in height. He seems to be getting kind of judgy now too. He didn't do very well last time Mom crashed. He was depressed the whole time she was gone, but back then Dhanu was a huge help.

"Calm down, I'll look for it, okay? Just please don't tell Mom."

"Well hurry," Jonah says. "Before someone else finds it first."

I give him the side eye, raise one eyebrow for effect.

"Maybe that would be a good thing," I tell him. "Maybe that ring is a reminder, and needs to be gone for good, so Mom can stop missing Dhanu so much and feeling so sorry for herself. You have to admit that ever since she left, our mother has so not been the same. Half the time she seems totally unfocussed, buzzing around the house, doing too much at once. And the other half she has this faraway look in her eyes as if she'd like to be anywhere else but here. She vanishes for hours, doesn't say where she's going or when she's coming back. I don't get it."

"I know. Same here," Jonah admits, as a shadow of anxiety crosses his face. "She's acting way too weird. And it's scaring me. I just want her to be okay. And since the ring seems so important to her right now, you NEED to find it. Please, Sophie. It might already be too late."

There's an echo of panic in his voice. Maybe he's right and the ring is important enough to our mom that she needs to have it back pronto. It's bad enough that our dad seems never to be home, always flying off on another business trip. And Dhanu was mom's backup. For fun we used to say that Dad had two wives. And Mom would correct us, saying that Dhanu was like having a best friend and a sister combined. The ring must mean a lot to her. And likewise, to my brother.

"Okay. Don't worry, Jonah. I promise I won't stop looking until I find it."

"Thanks Sophie," he murmurs, trying to smile. "I know I can always count on you."

Wow, I wish he hadn't said that. Talk about pressure. Fingers crossed that my promise won't be an impossible one to keep.

Chapter Two

Tara

I slump into the desk chair in my bedroom and fire up my ancient laptop. Why is my mom making this find-a-guy thing such a top priority? Aren't there more important things to worry about, like getting a job maybe? I try to forget about the possibility that Mom could be bringing this new guy home sometime soon. Because the last two times were a total disaster.

The first guy actually flirted with me the only time I met him. When he slipped an arm around my shoulder and squeezed a little too hard, Mom hoofed him out the door. And after just a couple of dates, the second jerk told Mom that she should send me somewhere for a sleepover so they could 'enjoy some quality time alone'. Yuck! Never saw him again either. But I know my mom is holding out for the real deal. There are tons of internet dating success stories, and she's desperate to be one of them herself.

To distract myself, I focus on the ring. Ever since I was little I've been attracted to glittery things. My nana used to call me a crow, because I loved looking through her jewelry box and trying on all the old rhinestone earrings and necklaces that she'd inherited from her own mother. After Nana died, my dad took them all to a pawn shop. Mom had no say in the matter, either. That was when their relationship crashed and burned for good.

Online that evening I learn all I can about moonstones. How they offer inspiration and intuitiveness to the wearer. How they bring good fortune, especially for girls and women. How placing one in moonlight could recharge it. It all sounds totally bunk to me. How could a gemstone possibly possess powers? The only power this one has over me is that I can't take my eyes off it. And that maybe I'm getting a little too obsessed.

I wear it to bed, fall asleep rubbing the stone with my fingertip, like Aladdin rubbed the magical lamp, and feel silly for even thinking it. And when I wake up in the middle of the night, I turn on my lamp and stare at the mesmerizing stone. Milky white, like a shimmering disk of moonlight with those two twinkling stars on either side.

How much did this ring mean to the person who was careless enough to lose it? It's clearly a woman's ring. Is she staring at her bare hand and wondering where she left it? Did she retrace her steps and search frantically once she realized it was gone? What is she thinking right now? Her thoughts can't possibly be as ridiculous as mine. She might even be sobbing into her pillow. Losing the ring might have even changed the direction of her life. Or is that possible?

I promise myself that I'll take it to the police station tomorrow. Right after school.

* * *

"So? What did you decide about the ring?" Priya asks me at my locker Friday morning.

Hmmm. I need to choose my words carefully. Because Priya is still looking at me in that strange way, as if she wonders if I'll do the right thing. And it's making me feel all funny inside.

"Don't worry, that's taken care of," I tell her, trying my best to sound convincing. "Hopefully nobody will claim it." I fumble around in my locker so she won't be able to see the guilt that's heating up my lying face.

"Oh, I doubt that will happen," she says. "Somebody out there must be going crazy wondering where they lost it. Probably cried all night."

When I spin around she's smiling at me. I grin at her. "Yeah, you're right. Guess I shouldn't get my hopes up, huh?"

"I knew you'd do the right thing, Tara," she says. "So, yet another rehearsal tonight.

Thank God it's Friday. My homework is taking a beating, and so is my sleep. I need to catch up."

"Oh, so you know what, Pri? I actually can't make it tonight," I tell her. "I forgot I have an appointment. But maybe we can get together on Saturday night and run through our lines. I wouldn't mind going over the Emily role, with you playing George, just in case, you know."

Right away I know this news isn't sitting well with my friend.

"An appointment, huh? Since when?" Her dark eyes are curious, but I shrug, don't offer a reason and try to hold her gaze in an innocent way. "Okay, so just give me a call and we can meet up at the coffee shop tomorrow." Then she nudges me. "Too bad you won't ever get to play that part. I've seen the way you stare at Silas, you know. So obvi!"

Gulp. Is it really that obvious? I always try my best not to be caught watching him, trying to pretend as if I don't care, unlike so many of the others. I nudge her back. "Speak for yourself," I say. "All the girls are guilty of that!"

Some more than others, I think as I hurry to my first class. It isn't hard to see that Priya is spellbound by the beautiful creature that is Silas. It's impossible to miss the dreaminess in her eyes whenever he's close by. I can tell she's letting her imagination run wild, probably daydreaming about a dream date. As far as learning lines, I know that she has his part memorized entirely, just by the way her lips move while he's speaking on stage. And I figure she knows the Emily lines as well as Iris does, wishing it could be her instead. She is crushing so hard on Silas.

But who isn't? He's quickly become the focal point of the entire drama club.

And me, well of everyone in this drama production, I'm probably the least obsessed with him. Because I have much bigger issues in my life. Adding a guy crush to the heap could only make matters worse. But I still can't help sneaking a glance now and then when I know he isn't looking my way. He sure is easy on the eyes, and sometimes I find myself imagining what it would be like to have a real boyfriend as cool as him some day, instead of fantasy ones.

Which is why it comes as a complete shock when someone grabs my sleeve as I'm rushing to class. When I snap my head around, quite prepared to slug that someone for startling me, Silas stares at me with his huge brown eyes. My heart does a backwards somersault, and something deep inside of me instantly starts to melt. So much for good intentions.

"Hey Tara! I just want to say congrats for being chosen as the Emily understudy."

He runs his fingers through his dark rumpled hair and smiles so wide and bright that I'm almost speechless. Silas has a face that stops you in your tracks, and he's actually talking to me. He actually knows my name. My heart is thudding major hard now. I'm sure he must be able to hear it. Wow, this changes everything. Sorry, not sorry, Priya.

"It's um, uh, very exciting," I manage to mumble. "Um, uh, well, you know, I think I almost know the part."

"That's excellent. Okay, so I was just wondering if maybe we could talk about..."

Over our heads the bell rings and I jump. If I don't hurry, I'll be late for class and the teacher will freak out. Plus, apparently I'm tongue tied, and sound like a complete jackass!

"Sorry, I have to get moving, Silas," I quickly tell him as I turn to make a dash for it.

I spin around so he won't catch a glimpse of my cheeks that are burning hot right now. Then his hand is on my arm again, so I take a deep breath and turn around slowly, faking calm while my insides are practically vibrating.

"I know. Me too, Sophie. But can I at least get your cell number," he says, offering me that sideways smile that makes all the girls crazy. Now I can't deny that it's starting to have the same effect on me. "So I can text you about something."

Ugh. I cringe. "Um...sorry. Don't have one. You have to call my home phone."

He actually looks shocked. I'm not exactly thrilled myself, but I'm dealing with it, and hope to talk Mom into letting me get one soon. "Land line?" he says. "Really?"

"Yup. It's in Canada411, under M. Kowalchuk." I wobble away on rubbery legs.

Of course I can't concentrate for the rest of the morning. For some reason Silas wants to contact me. No guy has ever contacted me before in my life. Sometimes I think that no guy ever will. But yikes, it finally happened. Then I realize I'm probably overthinking this. It's got to be about the play, as much as I wish that it wasn't, silly me. All the hope in the world won't actually make this happen for me. But wow, at least he talked to me, actually knows I'm alive.

At lunch time Priya notices how thoughtful I am and keeps watching me as I quietly chew on my cheese and lettuce sandwich and ignore the chatter from the rest of the girls at our table. I make sure I never make eye contact with Silas across the cafeteria either. I manage to sneak in a few peeks though, just can't help it. But he never looks my way once.

After school I take off before Priya can ask any more questions about my so-called 'appointment'. I already told the drama teacher, Ms. Wilding, in the hallway earlier today, that I have to miss rehearsal for 'personal reasons'. I could tell she was disappointed when her face fell, but there's still plenty of time for rehearsing. Shoving my guilt aside, I hurry home for my appointment—with the moonstone ring.

I'm almost starting to believe that the lovely glittering object does possess some sort of strange power over me. Nobody has a clue that I've been carrying it in my pocket all day, just to have it nearby. Reaching in to fiddle with it, reassure myself it's still there. Peeking while I'm in the washroom stall. I can't wait to get it on my finger again, to stare at that shiny stone nonstop.

I slip through the front door and head for my room. Mom is sitting at the kitchen table, sipping tea and scratching lottery tickets with what she calls her 'lucky dime'. Lucky, because earlier this year she won two hundred bucks while using it to scratch with. She actually gave me twenty bucks that time and treated me and her best friend Lyla to dinner at The Keg. Then she bought more tickets and the money was gone. Now that lucky dime is stored in a dainty fine China sugar bowl with hand-painted roses that once belonged to my nana, one of the few keepsakes that Dad didn't cash in at the pawn shop.

The tickets are scattered across the table. At three dollars apiece, I figure she must have wasted over twenty bucks today.

"Hi Mom." I try to slip past with just a nod.

"Hey sweetie," she says smiling. "No rehearsal?"

I shake my head, and head for the hall, but she grabs my hand and holds it tight.

"Fresh pot of Earl Gray tea and a bunch of tickets to scratch. Want to help? Maybe it's our lucky day." She has that shiny look in her eyes that happens whenever she has a new pile of tickets and high hopes.

I wince. I don't even have a good excuse this time.

"Seriously, Mom, you know I don't support this. I'd rather you wasted the money on a treat, like ordering pizza or Chinese, or something. It's just so pointless, isn't it?" But like a good daughter, I sit down with a gigantic sigh that I don't even try to hide. She slides over a card with a bunch of fruit symbols, and I start using my fingernail to scratch.

"Coins work better," says the seasoned pro.

"Whatever, Mom," I say, and bury my frustration in the boring scratch process.

A few minutes later I push the card back across the table.

"Okay, I scratched all the symbols and filled in one whole row. So does that mean anything, or do you have to fill in the whole stupid card?"

Mom's brows pop up and disappear under her dark bangs. "What?" She grabs the card. "Holy cow! But look, you haven't scratched out the dollar sign at the end of the row. To find out what the prize is worth."

"Oh God, this is totally lame, Mom!" I grab back the card, scratch it. And gasp.

"Seventy-five thousand dollars?" I can barely breathe. "Am I even seeing this right?"

"Shut. Up." Mom's hand is trembling when she picks up the card. She stares at it. Her eyes instantly flood with tears that dribble mascara down her cheeks. "I don't believe this, Tara," she whispers, blinking. "Can this really be happening?"

Then she leaps up, whips around the table and yanks me to my feet. And my mom actually starts spinning me in crazy circles as she lets out little shrieks of joy. It's contagious! I can't help adding a few whoops to the mix myself as we jump and twirl around the kitchen floor, bashing into chairs and laughing hysterically.

"Everything's going to change," she chirps, and it comes out like a song. "This is going to be like a whole new chapter for us, sweetie. A chance to start over again!"

"Can I finally get my own phone?" I shriek, taking advantage of this happy moment.

"Of course you can," she shrieks right back. "Your choice of phones too!"

"Yahoo!" I yell, and the two of us spin like a couple of whirlwinds around the room.

"We'll lease a car, and find a better place to live," Mom chants in her singsong voice. "We won't have to worry so much. We'll have a buffer. This is like a bolt from the blue, a gift from right out of..."

Then suddenly she freezes, her arms go limp and her face sags. Smeared mascara mixed with too much blusher makes her look like a demented clown. It's as if all the joy has drained right out of her. "Oh no, dammit, your dad cannot find out about this. He'll want a share for sure."

And all my sudden hope and joy trickles away.

* * *

Sophie

I hop on my bike and make a beeline to the main street where I get off the bus every day after school. Everything around me is a total blur. I can only focus on one thing. Finding that ring so our mom doesn't lose it completely. Sure, her magical thinking is driving me nuts, but better that than her falling into a pit of anxiety-fueled despair like she does now and then. Somehow having the ring gave her hope. Sounds crazy, but she's a bit crazy herself. Her whole life seems based on the fortunes of our father instead of digging deeper and creating her own life story.

It's only a short ride away, the stretch of sidewalk where I started running earlier today to try to make it home just in case 'he' was outside bouncing. I drop my bike on somebody's lawn and start pacing back and forth with my eyes glued to the ground, trying to catch a glimpse of something sparkling in the sunshine. No sign of it. So, I walk my bike all the way home, scanning the ground the entire time. Absolutely no luck. Some lucky moonstone. Jonah's voice echoes in my brain. 'Hurry, before someone else finds it first.' Looks like it's already too late.

I can hear the basketball bouncing off the pavement before I even turn the corner onto our street. There he is in the driveway, slam dunking, completely focused. Looks as if he's talking to himself again, too. So weird, like he's always giving himself a pep talk so he'll do a better job at sinking baskets, or something. He must be a star player on his school team. I know he doesn't go to the same private school as me and Jonah. Not many families around here can afford the luxury. And besides, I definitely would have noticed.

His face is a rare miracle of nature.

Our new neighbours just moved in earlier this year when the snow was flying back in January. I don't even know their names yet. All I've been able to manage is finger waves and a smile. One of these days I need to find the courage to actually introduce myself. But he barely even glances my way, always concentrating with a dazed look in his eyes, ever since he ventured out into the driveway when it finally warmed up last week after a miserably long winter.

"Hey there neighbour," I stutter out, and try another feeble wave. Hey there *neighbour*! Did I really just say something so dumb? Luckily he didn't even hear me over the constant thumping of his basketball on the driveway. I slink back inside my house, feeling defeated.

In the kitchen, Mom is trying to scrape together something that looks like dinner but I'm not sure I want to risk eating it. Whenever Dhanu had a day off, our mother would just leave it up to us to pull something together for meals. Usually Kraft Dinner, of course. With weenies. Some baby carrots on the side. Covering all the important food groups.

"What are you whipping up for dins today, Mom?"

"Oh, hi honey. I didn't even hear you go out. I'm working on a pot pie. I found a few recipes online. You use leftover meat, whatever kind you want. Add it to gravy, along with veggies. Then you make a crust with this baking mix, and lay it on top, and bake the whole works in the oven. The pictures look delicious. All I could find in the freezer was some breakfast sausage and frozen peas and carrots though, and I have gravy mix, so I gave it a shot anyway."

Sausages? Gross! "Cool," I tell her, peering at the concoction in the saucepan that she keeps stirring. "It looks sort of good." Wrong, it looks as if someone threw up in that pot after eating a bad weenie. Ugh. Why did I even think that? How will I ever be able to eat it now?

I actually do feel kind of sorry for our mother, as she struggles to get along without Dhanu in her life anymore. And our dad who is practically never around, and who, I'm pretty sure, actually plans it that way. I've been wondering about Dad more and more lately, ever since he started being home with us even less than before. But I always chase the thoughts away.

"I can't stop thinking about that ring, Sophie," Mom says, and when she spins around, she has that look on her face. A look of zero emotion. Her voice sounds flat right now too. I hope she's not tumbling again, into that bottomless pit that comes with her depressive episodes. It's been a while, but I've seen it coming ever since Dhanu left.

Mom wound up on a psych ward once for a couple of weeks, after she stopped eating and wouldn't stop crying for days on end; she was shattered inside because of our dad. And her disturbing absence is an awful episode in our lives that Jonah and I would both prefer to forget. Her permanent head meds don't seem to be doing the job well now, though. Her moods fluctuate so much lately, sometimes elated and other times defeated. I'm so afraid that she might be teetering on a dangerous fence, and I'm terrified about which side she's going to wind up falling on.

"It's gonna turn up Mom, so don't worry, okay. For sure you left it somewhere."

"But where?" Her chin starts to tremble. "I'll feel so bad if I lost it. Because it's all I have left of Dhanu. Just to look at it and think about her and remember all the lovely times we had with her way back when. She used to take care of everything for me, for us. I trusted her completely. I didn't even have to make decisions whenever your dad was away. She made them all for me. And then everything changed...and...then I..." She swallows hard, breathes deep.

"Yeah, well maybe that wasn't such a good thing, Mom," I tell her, and her face drops and some tears slide out, which just rattles me even more. "Sorry for being harsh, but honestly, it's like you don't even want to try. Why not make your own decisions for a change? I know you can do this if you really work on it. You need to learn to rely on yourself a lot more now."

"Sophie," she half sobs. "You have no idea. And I'm doing my best here you know."

Hand to her heart as if she's mortally wounded not just slightly insulted. How is this crushing her so hard? What is the big deal about this stupid ring and losing her housekeeper anyway? I mean, we aren't little kids anymore. It's not like she really even needs her at this point.

That's another one of her tragic flaws. Every little thing becomes way too big an issue. I guess it's just a part of who she is, or at least who she was. And drama is embedded in her soul, for sure. Sometimes she gets this starry look in her eyes and reminisces about her high school and university days when she was in every school play production. Started out acting in small roles then getting the lead. In those days, around twenty years back, she was seriously thinking about pursuing acting as a career. Just before she met Dad and married young, that is. Then, oops, had me right away and Jonah eighteen months later. Sometimes I think she still resents us for screwing up her plans.

"I don't really think you are, you know. In fact, coming up with this pot pie is probably one of the most momentous decisions I've ever seen you make. Yay for you!"

"That sounded a lot like sarcasm," Mom tells me in a suddenly blunt tone. "And right now, I've decided to ignore you and finish making dinner."

"Again, yay for you! Go Mom!" I snatch a banana from the bowl on the counter and head for my bedroom.

Where I instantly start guilt tripping for being so mean to my mom. She's clearly going through something intense right now, and missing her sweet Dhanu, who became her confidante, and always helped her through all her household dilemmas. Come to think of it, maybe she would appreciate hearing from Dhanu right about now. Come to think of it, I haven't heard from her myself lately, since I got an email just after she left early last month. Maybe I need to let her know how much Mom is missing her. Maybe that would cheer her up a bit.

I sit down at my laptop and compose a quick note, hoping she'll read it soon and send Mom a message of hope or something. Of course I can't mention a word about the missing ring. Can't even remind Dhanu that she gave it to Mom, in case she asks about it.

Hey Dhanu, missing you tons. Know who else is? Frances! She's been so down lately, can't seem to get over you being gone. And with Dad away so much, it's almost like a double whammy for her. For me too. I miss our 'sister friend' sessions in my room. Hanging out together and talking about silly stuff like celebrity gossip. You helping me sort through my friend issues. Me helping you with online shopping. Such fun times.

I hope all's well with your 'amma'. I hope she's feeling better, and you can come back here someday. So, I was wondering if you would maybe drop a note to Mom. Like I said, she hasn't been herself at all lately, and Jonah and I are worried. Maybe you can find a way to help her move on and get past the fact that you're gone now. And that she can make it without you. And tell her you'll come back and visit whenever you can.

Hope you get to have some good times in between helping your mom. Sending love to your whole family! Thanks!
xoxo Sophie

I press send and start peeling my banana, then spot Jonah lurking in my doorway.

"Any luck?" he says, first thing and with a too hopeful voice.

"Nope," I tell him. "That sucker is gonzo. Want a hunk of banana? This one is huge!"

"No. No banana. That's all you've got, Sophie? Gonzo? Well, you have to make it un-gonzo. You have to try and find it. I feel really sorry for Mom right now."

"Well so do I, Jonah. I even emailed Dhanu and asked her to get in touch with Mom in case that might cheer her up. I don't know what else we can do for her."

"That's not enough. You need to do more about the ring. Put up a sign or something. Or Mom might lose it completely. She seems so on the edge right now."

"Lose it because of a ring? I doubt that. It's not about the ring. It's about her magical thinking. And about her denial. This ring thing is the least of her problems. She needs to snap out of her sadness daze and move on. And maybe Dhanu can walk her through it when she emails Mom. I mean, it's not like she really even needed Dhanu anymore, right?"

"Still, you owe her that much. You need to put up a sign, Sophie. I figured you wouldn't find the ring, so I made you some of these."

My brother hands me a few sheets of paper. He's made me some signs, in huge letters. Like you sometimes see taped to light posts, advertising guitar lessons, or cleaning ladies, or dog walkers.

$$$ LOST / REWARD $$$
MOONSTONE RING WITH TWO DIAMONDS
SENTIMENTAL VALUE

My cell phone number is repeated in vertical lines along the bottom, hanging in little strips to tear off.

"Nobody is turning in that ring," I tell him bluntly. "Nobody is that honest."

"Yes they are. You need to go back and staple these signs to poles along the street. In case there's a chance someone happens to find it. Lots of people want to do the right thing, you know."

Wow, he's so naïve. "Oh God, you're going to guilt me into doing this, aren't you?"

"Yeah, I am, Sophie. I hate it when Mom gets all weird and obsessed. And right now, it's all about the ring. And you know that things will only get worse if she doesn't find it. Remember what happened last time her brain went bye-bye."

"Okay, okay, don't even remind me. You're getting all weird now too. I'll do it tomorrow morning, okay? I don't have time to go back there tonight. Got a book report to finish."

"Whatever," Jonah tells me. "But it's not fair to Mom, is it? You did something stupid, and now you have to find a way to undo it, before she loses it."

He thrusts the signs in my face. With a snarl I snatch them from his hand, then he spins around and stalks out of my room. Right away I start working on this *Lord of the Flies* book report I've been putting off for too long. And trying to keep my mind off the fact that I might have screwed my mom up by snatching that ring and thinking I was doing her a favour. Bad idea, as it turns out, but I'd never admit that out loud.

One thing that does turn out okay is her sausage pot pie. Nice golden crust with thick gravy bubbling out through little vent holes she poked into the top with a fork. Lots of nice chunks of sausage, along with peas and carrots. It's so delicious that the three of us devour the whole thing. Which must be a first, and a milestone for our mother.

"Mom, seriously, this rivals anything that Dhanu ever made for us," I tell her, trying to force a smile out of her, to erase that gloomy look of woe that seems permanently glued to her face these days. Seems only that stupid ring has been able to make her smile lately.

"Really?" she says, lips curling upward slightly. "You're not just saying that to be nice, right Sophie?"

"Well maybe, but it's really true, Mom. I mean, for your early efforts, this is one of the best yet. And I'm sure that you'll just keep right on acing this."

"And I'm on my third helping," Jonah reminds her. "When have I ever eaten this much of anything we've ordered from Uber Eats even? This is epic." He scoops up gravy with his fingertip and licks it off."

"You'd eat pretty much anything that was drowned in gravy though, right Jonah?" I remind him. "If you get my drift."

Jonah's wide grin is contagious when he flips me the bird. And Mom's first for-real smile in ages is the brightest part of my whole day so far. I hope for the sake of our whole family, that she's on her way out of her latest slump.

* * *

Friday morning, I sleep in too long, and Mom doesn't remind me like she usually does by yelling up the stairs. While I'm scrambling to wash and dress, I can detect a delicious aroma drifting up the stairs. It's so amazing that my stomach actually starts grumbling. Bacon for sure. Heavenly. Haven't smelled that in forever. Dhanu never cooked bacon for us. We respected the fact that she wasn't into pork. Pancakes and bacon for breakfast? Shocker! Mom seems to be making a serious effort to do her own cooking, trying out online recipes more than ever now. Thank God. I've been craving home cooked meals, and this week they've finally started to happen. But the burning question is, how come Mom suddenly seems more motivated these days? So bizarre!

After a mad dash for the bus, and making it just in time for the bell, it's hard to concentrate at school. I hand in my book report in first period English Lit. Try to focus as Mr. Mills drones on and on. In my lap, my phone vibrates, and I glance down guardedly. Phones are mostly a no-no in our classrooms unless they become part of the assignment. But since Mr. Mills lectures in a trance with his eyes half shut, he won't even notice me checking my screen.

A text from my BFF Lexi. She sits a couple of rows back.

Well, did you talk to him yet?

No. And shut up about it Lex.

Lame, is her response.

She's been on my case about the new neighbour ever since she spotted him for the first time last week. And she's been threatening to make the first move if I don't do it myself. She sends me a few more texts which I ignore, then I finally turn off my phone so I can't even be tempted to look. As far as friends go, she's probably the most pushy and, dare I even think it, bullying of all the girls I chill with. She has a way of making you do things you'd never imagined doing, ever. Yet everyone just keeps right on letting her, and never asking why. Including me.

But how do you ditch your oldest friend for fear of how she'll react if you speak up and call her out for something dumb that she does? I know I'm way too forgiving, but I have a soft spot for Lexi. As nasty as she acts sometimes, she always manages to find a way to be there for me in some bizarre way or other. Just when I'm about ready to give up on her completely, she'll come up with a sweet way of making me feel better. So, I can never be certain if she's perfectly diabolical or perfectly righteous. And I just keep on hanging around to find out.

Dhanu always said that you can never know what someone might be carrying deep in their soul. Or what secrets they're hiding in their hearts. Meaning you have to try your best to be forgiving and understanding, I guess. To try being kind to people, since you can never know their circumstances or what might have made them the way they are. Basically, Dhanu figured we all have a backstory that affects us going forward. Not everyone is able to face their inner demons, or how they might have been affected by their own life story. But wow, it's way easier to just be judgy, instead of stopping to think about all this complicated stuff first. I figure the only demons Lexi has are way too much money and privilege, and parents too busy to notice. The reality is everything she takes for granted isn't going away any time soon. So, is she lucky, or doomed?

"Sophie, I've called your name three times. Are you still on the planet or has your brain been hijacked by your imagination again? Hello in there!"

Oh crap. When I snap out of my daze, everyone is staring at me with half grins on their faces. Jacob has his phone out, filming this. Ugh. Yep I was deep in thought again. And I guess I missed something because Mr. Mills has questions in his eyes.

"Sorry sir, I'm still on the planet," I murmur to my desk. Everyone titters a little. Way too often I honestly wish I could go to a public school, and not this private one where it feels like everyone judges you nonstop. And nothing that happens ever goes away.

The rest of the day doesn't really improve much. It doesn't much matter because I can't focus on anything ever since I discovered the sheaf of signs and the stapler in my backpack that I totally forgot about in my rush to get to school. Which means time wasted in trying to find the ring. What if the person who found it sold it already? And never got a chance to see the sign along with the offer of a reward. It could already be too late to get it back.

Which is why I slip out of class quickly and skip going to my locker so I can catch the first bus home. On Friday after school, everyone usually hangs around to make weekend plans and flirt. Not me today, no time to get sucked into that game. I make it to the stop just as the early bus pulls up, and I'm on my way with a couple of others before the big crowd shows up.

As soon as I get off the bus fifteen minutes later, I whip out those signs and start stapling them up on posts along the way home. And making plans to be reading out on my front porch, which I never do, just in case basketball boy decides to shoot hoops after school today.

No lucky ring in my pocket but maybe I'll get lucky anyway.

Chapter Three

Tara

As I stare at the winning ticket in her hand, I'm not sure if I should feel elated or terrified. Mom is right, but I don't want to believe that it could even be possible. If Dad drops back into our lives right now, then everything could fall apart again, including my sad, unstable mom.

"What do you mean? How would Dad find out? And why would he even get any?"

"They'll post my picture on the lottery website. And he's always checking numbers to see if he won. You remember how he used to buy tickets all the time, and I made sure that I always signed them." Her hand is on her neck now as she stares at the ticket. She swipes away her tears. "And we're not even legally separated, right? Quick. Grab me a pen."

"But he never signed this ticket, Mom. And he's always behind on his support payments," I remind her. "He owes us tons. And anyway, this is your money, not his." I rifle through the junk drawer in the counter behind me, dig out a pen and slide it over.

"I don't know the rules when it comes to prize winning." She quickly signs the back of the scratch card. "I'm not even sure if, since we're not even legally separated, he's entitled to a cut. There. Signed. Now we have to get to a lottery prize center and claim this money ASAP. Maybe he won't even find out about it." She sucks in a deep breath, her eyes wide and determined for a fleeting instant. "Fingers crossed."

"You mean it, Mom? This is actually gonna change things?"

I don't want to get my hopes up too high, just to have them demolished again. The possibility of change is impossible to imagine! Mom has started to tremble, seems so overcome with the sudden possibilities of everything this could mean. I give her a hard hug and she hugs me back.

Mom's face crumples with emotion again when she nods. "This is a good start." She sighs long and loud. "Maybe I can finally get on with my life. This could be the jump start I need. You're my lucky charm today, sweetie. From now on you get to scratch all the tickets I buy."

"Lucky charm, huh? Oka-y-y-y," I say. "But maybe you won't have to buy anymore."

Mom is distracted now, on her feet, grabbing for the phone. "Don't tell a soul. And I mean absolutely nobody. I don't want people coming out of the woodwork."

"So, who are you calling?"

"Lyla, of course. She's my best friend. She's always stuck by me. It's okay to tell her, right? She needs to be the first to know." She's so excited, it's like her fingers are on speed dial. She's on such an emotional roller coaster right now.

I swallow hard. The moonstone ring is in my pocket. And I don't want to go there, to even risk believing that it might actually be true, that it really could bring good fortune. Even though everything I've read about online hints at the possibility that it works. I don't want to think that I'm actually that gullible.

But clearly, something has already started to change!

Mom orders Thai for dinner, the most expensive dishes on the menu. And we totally pig out. Meanwhile, she makes plans. Tomorrow she'll call a limo cab, and ride in style to the lottery centre to pick up her cheque. So much for keeping it secret. She wants to do it alone, to feel the rush of this experience all for herself. I'm okay with that. She still isn't sure what to do with all that money yet, either. But she guarantees she'll figure it out pretty fast once she talks to the people at the bank. I hope she makes the right decisions about her windfall. I have a few ideas myself about how the two of us should best spend all that money. *Just* the two of us.

And then, joy of joys, she promises we can go over to the mall and buy me a smart phone tomorrow, since now she can finally afford to pay for a plan. I can't believe that at long last I'll finally have one, that I can actually catch up with the rest of this techno-obsessed world. I'm going to be connected to my friends! I plan on installing every social media app possible as soon as my phone is out of the box.

The land line rings a while later when I'm finally in my room staring at the sparkly moonstone ring under my desk lamp. I grab the phone without even checking call display.

"Is this Tara ?" A guy's voice? Seriously?

"Yup, that's me." By that point my heart is already throbbing in my throat. Because it couldn't possibly be him. Could it? I'd never be that lucky. Would I?

"Hey. So, it's Silas. Symonds. You know, from the drama production."

Oh my God! As if he has to explain. Which he must have been doing because I haven't answered him yet. I'm still too gobsmacked to even speak. It's as if my tongue has gone totally numb. Then finally the words come spilling out. Probably too many of them.

"Oh cool. So nice to hear from you. I never thought you'd call. How's it going, bud?" How's it going *bud*? Did I really just say that? What a dork I am!

"*Bud*?" he says, then starts laughing. "You crack me up, Tara."

"Do I?" Whew! "So, what's up anyway?" I wish my voice wasn't trembling so much. Never in my life has a guy called me. Never ever! I'm instantly jittery, so afraid of saying the wrong thing again. I can even feel myself blushing to the point that my cheeks are sizzling hot.

"So anyway, I noticed you weren't at rehearsal today."

"Uh yeah, because I had an...appointment." This lie for the sake of the ring is coming back to haunt me already. And it's too late to put it back into the box it escaped from.

"Everything's coming together. Iris and I are getting the lines right without prompts now, really feeling the part. And the blocking's going great too."

Iris and the *Our Town* 'Emily Webb' role that I secretly covet.

"Good to hear." Awkward silence. "Um...so...what else is up?"

"Do you know all your lines yet? For the Emily role. You know, in case Iris gets sick?"

I almost have it nailed. But lately I've been a bit distracted by that glimmering bauble I've been carrying everywhere. "Yeah, I'm getting there. Ms. Wilding says she wants to do a run through with me playing the part at some point."

"Definitely a good idea. Just in case. Anyway, I was wondering if maybe you'd like to get together with me tomorrow night. You know, to go over the part, run lines. Maybe we could meet over at Starbucks or something. We've got to get it right, you and me."

Meet for coffee! Yikes! Silas Symonds is actually asking to meet up with me! How could this even be happening? I don't know how to talk to a guy Silas's age! Just the thought of it makes those butterflies madly dance in my belly. For an instant I'm so tongue-tied that words won't come out. Is there even the slightest chance that he...he can't possibly like me but...no way...

"Yoo hoo? You still there, Tara ?" Silas asks.

"Oh, uh sorry, yes, sure Silas, I guess, maybe we could get together some time. I was kind of going to meet up with Priya at Starbucks on Saturday night. She's expecting to hang out with me, so I don't know..." Oh my God, don't you know when to shut up, Tara?

"Okay then. Well, I guess I'll see you at school next week. Later Tara." He hangs up.

Actually hangs up on me before I can even try to explain myself. Which makes me utterly crazy. I can't believe I've already blown it with a guy I'm secretly crushing on. When I have a perfectly good excuse to hang out with him. I really do need to practice this part so I can get it right, if by some remote chance I actually need to fill in for Iris. I have to get up my nerve, to face Silas, to be brave enough to step into the Emily role with confidence. And not become a tongue-tied fool. Either that, or I'll have to give up the part entirely. Because I could never risk freezing up on stage and ruining the play for everyone. Silas is right. We need to practice together. What an idiot I'm starting to become. And when did I start doubting myself so much anyway?

"Oh Tara ," I say to the moonstone ring. "Quit over-thinking everything. You'll do just fine if you have to play opposite Silas. And anyway, get real. There has got to be an ulterior motive. He was probably just asking you for coffee to make sure you really know your lines. Take a deep breath and believe in yourself."

That night I fall asleep wearing the moonstone ring again. It's already beginning to feel like an indispensable part of my body, a part of my whole being.

* * *

By late Saturday afternoon Mom's cheque is in the bank, and I have my first cell phone. As soon as it's activated, I text Priya. We've already arranged to meet at the local Starbucks tonight after dinner to run lines and cue each other whenever we miss any. That coffee shop has turned into a sort of weekend meet-up place for weirdo kids like us who aren't into drinking and partying but prefer to hang out with like-minded friends and to sip on a different sort of expensive beverage. Caramel lattes are my absolute favourite. Even though I can barely afford them on my meagre weekly allowance.

Guess who?

The first two words I've ever texted in my life. Unreal!

Who IS this??????

The very first reply I ever got on my very first cell phone. Cool!

Don't forget. Starbucks @ 7!!!! I text back.

IS THIS YOU TARA ????? SERIOUSLY????

I don't reply to that one. More fun to just keep her guessing for a bit before I take off to meet her. And I can't wait to get out of the house. I'm tempted to hide the ring inside my pillow case before leaving. I can't risk losing it, and I sure can't let Priya find out that I actually still have it. But instead, I stick it in my pocket, because what if it has to be with you in order for the moonstone's charm to keep on working. Hah, as if!

Mom told me her new beau is coming to pick her up later, and I'm not ready to meet him yet, which is why I need to be gone. I'm not sure I'll ever be ready after the last two turned out so badly. She told me they're going out for dinner. And at least Mom was sweet enough to make me some tuna melts before I leave. She has been in an incredibly good mood for the last twenty four hours. I only hope it lasts as long as the money does.

I'm just about to head for the front door, when I hear the sharp rap from my bedroom through our too-thin walls. Someone at the front door! Oh God, don't tell me he's early. Then I hear the door creaking open.

"Oh hi, Dave! You're early! Wow! What gorgeous flowers? Are they for me?" Mom's voice is high and chirpy and ecstatic. I haven't heard her sound so animated in ages.

"Well, who else would they be for, Marie," says Dave's voice. "Congratulations, lucky lady! You lead a charmed life. First you met me, and now this."

I hear mom giggling.

No. Please say she didn't tell him. She couldn't possibly be clueless enough to start blabbing about her winning ticket to someone she barely even knows. Could she?

"Yeah, I'm having a lucky streak," I hear her say with a smile in her voice.

"You know, you really don't have to treat me to dinner tonight," Dave tells her.

"But I want to treat you, so you can help me celebrate," Mom says. "And I'm glad you're early. Tara hasn't gone out yet."

"You mean I finally get to meet your daughter? Great," he says.

I swallow hard, feel like climbing out my window and making a run for it. What is my mother even thinking! She made such a big deal about warning me not to tell a soul? Now there are two people who know about her win. Lyla, and this new Dave guy. I wonder how many others she's blabbed it to already. And what will stop the news from spreading as more random people find out about it? I grit my teeth and stride down the hall, so angry that I feel as if I might burst into flames any second.

"Seeya later Mom, I half growl." My hand is on the doorknob. I don't even glance toward the living room where they're sitting.

"Tara, wait a sec. Come and meet Dave Petrie," she chirps in an unnatural voice.

I'm not so sure I'm ready for this new version of my mom that I'm starting to see. This lady that always seems to be smiling too wide and acting too nice. To me it already feels way too phony. I'm more used to a mom that spends her time more frustrated than happy. One who complains a lot and barely even half-smiles.

This new mom is totally messing up my head.

"Sorry folks, in a rush, gotta fly." I poke my head in and wave to the guy, can see the two of them mostly in a blur. Gross, they're holding hands and sitting way too close to each other already. Chunky Monkey, are the words that come to mind when I see the stocky fellow sitting there grinning at me. Which is so mean, really. But this is pressing all the wrong buttons for me and my thoughts are going in too many nasty directions.

"Well clearly you inherited your good looks from your mom," he says.

No. He did *not* really say that, did he? What a dweeb! These guys she's been finding online would say just about anything to endear themselves to my mom and me. And to inch a little closer to her heart. And now, also to her cash windfall. It's the perfect plan.

"Wow, cool," I say, and head for the door and temporary freedom.

Gross. A new guy in our lives. One who reminds me of a ventriloquist puppet. Who's saying out loud everything he knows that Mom wants to hear the most. Anything that'll make her fall for him, of course. No doubt about it. I despise him already.

* * *

Sophie

Okay, so he isn't even out there yet when I get home to an empty house. I just wonder for a split second where Mom can possibly be out wasting money today. I take a deep breath and remind myself that I'm early, so I probably beat basketball boy home. Plus, maybe he hangs out at his public high school on Fridays the way we do at our private one.

In my bedroom I do my best to make myself look good without being too obvious. I touch up my mascara and grey eyeshadow that compliments my eyes. I dab on some plum lip gloss and smack my lips together in the mirror then check out my hair. Ugh. Not much I can do right now with my fake-sun-streaked blonde-brown 'horse tail', as my hair stylist describes it. I try a ponytail, which just says I'm-too-lazy no matter how hard I try adjusting it. So instead, I leave it loose around my shoulders after using the curling iron, then put on a cute velvet hairband.

Ah but what to wear? I'm 'blessed with' long slim legs and narrow hips, which a lot of my too-hippy grade eleven girlfriends hate me for. Little do they know that I wish I had some extra meat on my chicken legs. Thigh gaps aren't always a blessing. Skinny jeans, and a long loose yoga top will work in this case. Which I don't have, so I go into Mom's room and take one out of her dressing-room closet. I know how much she loves this creamy silky beauty that she paid way too much for. And with luck I'll have it back on the padded hanger before she even gets home.

I need to seem very nonchalant for my plan to work. Sitting out on the front porch in the fake wicker chair, with my feet up on the fake wicker footstool. Sipping a cold drink and fake reading. Perfect. I poke around in the fridge until I find a carton of chocolate milk which has been there awhile. It's only a few days past expiry, so I fill up a glass and drop in some ice cubes. Then I grab a book off the bookshelf in the den that's just off the kitchen. Any old book. Doesn't even matter. I pick a nice thick one, so maybe basketball boy will think I'm smart. But what if he doesn't like smart girls? Oh well, doesn't matter. I don't even know his name yet. I tuck the book under my arm, grab the glass of chocolate milk and my phone and head out to the front porch to stake out his house. Am I being a stalker, I wonder for just a second before brushing off that thought.

I've just settled in my chair and started scrolling through TikTok when I spot Jonah heading home from school. Oh no. Please don't let him stand out here talking to me.

"Wow, you're here already," he says. "You must have made the first bus." Then his eyes grow narrow, and he grins at me. "Ah, and you're sitting out here on the porch, like you *never* do. I get it now."

"Get what, Jonah," I say, glaring at him. "The only thing you should be getting is lost."

"You're waiting for him, aren't you. Oh Sophie, you are so obvious."

"Shut up. What does a grade ten kid know about this stuff anyway? Don't you have a refrigerator to raid or something? Can't you just be a typical fifteen-year-old and scrounge for snacks when Mom isn't home?"

"Good idea. And good luck. And speaking of luck, did you ever put up those signs?"

"Yes I did, Daddy," I tell him in a little girl voice. "I'm surprised you missed them."

"Guess I was staring at my phone while I was walking home from the bus," he admits.

Over his shoulder I can see a bike coming along the street. And I can tell from the red ball cap that it's *him*.

"I think I saw a slice of leftover pizza in the fridge from the other night, Jonah. Can you go in and grab it for me? I'm starved."

"Pizza? Sorry. Calling dibs on it." He slams right through the door. Perfect.

Basketball boy wheels up to the side of his house. God, he looks good. Heads must turn wherever he goes. Knees of girls everywhere must buckle at the sight of him. So many breaths must be drawn. And he lives right next door to me! Now's my chance except I have no clue where to start. In fact, every bit of feminine wiles I should possess at this age is missing in action.

"Hey there, how are you?" is the best I can come up with.

He looks over at me and my heart dances. Those dark-roast coffee coloured eyes are just so mesmerizing. And then he smiles wide and bright, and my heart is instantly sold.

"Hey, how's it going neighbour?" He leans his bike against his garage wall and takes a couple of steps toward me, and I'm tongue tied again.

"It's going good. So, I guess you're into basketball huh. I see you out here a lot." Okay not bad for starters, though still a bit lame, stating the obvious.

"Yeah," he says nodding. "It helps me concentrate. The repetitive bouncing and stuff. It's like white noise. Keeps me focused."

"Oh yeah, I know exactly what you mean." No, I totally don't. "So welcome to the neighbourhood, anyway. Is what I wanted to say. Since it's only just started getting warm out and I never had the chance before. You know...to..." My voice starts fading as I run out of more non-clever words. Why does this guy stuff have to be so freaking hard? Shouldn't it just come naturally?

"Yeah." He nods again, shakes his dark mane. "The never-ending winter. So, what are you reading anyway? I love a good book."

Ah. A reader. Cool, I made the right choice, coming out here with a novel. I hold it up for him, then see the back cover for the first time. *Fifty Shades of...* oh crap.

"Um this?" It comes out as a question. And I want to run inside to hide under my bed.

"Oh," he says as his eyebrows fly up. "Interesting choice."

"Yeah, um, I guess. We all need distractions sometimes, right?" Oh for the love of God! As my face burns brighter than a red dwarf star, I flash him my best smile, which I've practiced in the mirror, then take a quick gulp of chocolate milk. Which is so totally sour and chunky and gross that I instantly spurt it right back out and of course it sprays all down the front of my mom's favourite top.

"Oh shit," I yelp. "I need to clean this off. Seeya round sometime." And I flee into the house without even looking back, because I'm so freaking embarrassed, half-tripping over the doorstep in my hurry to disappear. Now he must think I'm some sort of klutzy, sloppy, sex-crazed maniac.

Then I realize that I still don't even know his name. How will I ever face him again?

Somehow or other I manage to wash out the chocolate milk from Mom's top before she gets home and dry it out with my blow dryer. The stain is like a very light shadow. Hopefully she won't even notice.

She shows up around seven with a bucket of takeout chicken and fries for supper and avoids answering the question when Jonah keeps asking her where she was all day. She's all quiet while she eats, but she keeps gulping white wine. Funny thing, too. As we all sit there in awkward silence, I realize that she hasn't even mentioned the missing ring once, like she's been doing the last couple of days. Which makes me think that maybe she's moving on and if it never turns up, then she won't freak out too much.

After chowing down on too much greasy food, I spend the rest of Friday in my room watching AppleTV on my tablet and texting with Lexi about how badly I blew it, then doing a video chat. She mostly laughs and shames me during the whole call.

"I mean seriously, Soph, you really have no clue how to talk to a guy, do you?" she keeps on saying. "You still haven't learned how to reel one in, after three years of high school, without an epic fail every time! What is even up with that! Have I taught you nothing at all?"

"Yeah, okay, I get it," I tell her before ending the call. "Just please, don't share this!"

And it utterly sucks, because why did I even bother to tell her about it in the first place? Just to be reminded and humiliated by the vastness of my own ineptitude. So, after that I mainly feel sorry for myself even more for blowing it so brutally with basketball boy.

Ugh. What an idiot.

* * *

By Saturday morning I'm feeling a little better. The guy isn't going anywhere soon, and I'm sure I'll have plenty of chances to explain myself once I finally get to know him. Someday we'll just laugh about it, then he'll take my face in his big strong hands, and cup my chin. Then he'll look into my eyes and kiss me long and sweet and gentle. And then he'll get down on one knee, and with a very earnest look in his eye...Okay! Enough with the pointless daydreams already.

Since school's out in less than two months, I have a lot on the go as far as essay writing and studying. Which is why I've planned to spend most of Saturday holed up in my room trying to get a ton done so I can maybe go out Saturday evening without feeling guilty. A lot of us hang out at a local Timothy's Coffee on Saturdays since we can't get into clubs yet and nobody's rich parents can be bothered hosting parties that mess up their picture perfect homes.

Just as I'm starting to make some headway on an essay, there's a very soft rap on my bedroom door. It's so quiet in fact, that I ignore it the first time, until the second knock sounds a bit more quick and urgent. When I call out 'what', the door opens slowly.

My brother is standing there. His eyes are open wide, and he looks more stunned than usual for a Saturday morning.

"What? What is your problem? Why is your mouth hanging open?"

Jonah puts a finger to his lips and sidles over to my desk. He has his phone clenched in his hand.

"I need to show you something. But don't even say a word or yell or anything, okay. Just look and keep your mouth shut."

"Wow, over dramatic or what. You are *so* Mom!" I tell him and he rolls his eyes and hands me his phone.

I'm looking at an Instagram photo on the screen. There are two people locked in a tight embrace, a sprawling field of flowers behind them. "So, who is this anyway? Are you creeping random strangers now?" But when I take a closer look, I gasp. "What the f..."

"Shut up Sophie," he hisses at me.

"What is this, though? And how did you even find it?" I swallow hard. "And is that really who I think it is?"

I'm looking at a photo of our dad. In Amsterdam. He's standing in a field of tulips with his arms around a woman and he's kissing her cheek. And she's smiling radiantly. And the woman is Dhanu. My whole body feels drained of blood, and I stand up and start pacing as I stare at the photo, unable to tear my eyes away.

"What is *happening*? Why are they together? How did you even find this? If Mom finds out she'll completely lose it and wind up back on the psyche ward like last time when she accused Dad of cheating on her."

"I know, I know! And I found this for the weirdest reason. You know how they suggest friends on Instagram? Anyway, this face showed up and I recognized the name as that woman that Dad works with in banking, who lives in Amsterdam, what's her name, Inger, I think. And so, I clicked on her face for some reason and started scrolling through photos of Amsterdam on her account. And bam, there it was! Posted like just last week, too.”

His eyes are wide and filled with dread. His mouth is opening and closing like a fish. Is he even breathing? This can only be a very bad thing in every way.

“But why is Dhanu in Amsterdam? Or maybe the photo was taken here sometime and Dad sent it to Inger.”

“Really Sophie? Really?” Now my brother is shaking his head way too hard, as if somehow it will make every nasty thought jamming up his brain right now go flying out through his ears.

Still in denial, I take a closer look. In the background I can see all of the clues though. You can’t mistake Amsterdam for anywhere else in the world, really. I’ve seen enough photos that Dad has sent us on his many travels. Plus, windmills! Why the hell is Dhanu with him in Amsterdam? When she’s supposed to be back home in Sri Lanka taking care of her ailing mother. And then, I know why, of course.

“So, she was lying all along,” I murmur. “And is Dad’s whole life a lie? He must have been carrying on with her here, and they cooked up this whole scheme so she could travel with him whenever he’s away. Or maybe he set her up in an apartment there since he has to be there for weeks on end and his salary is grossly huge. It’s the perfect ploy.”

I feel sick inside. Jonah's face is a sickly white now too, and he has tears in his eyes when he slowly sinks to my bed. He starts to chew his thumbnail. I hate seeing him distressed like this.

"Any wonder Mom and I haven't heard from Dhanu lately," I tell him. "Crap, and I just sent her an email asking her to get in touch with Mom to cheer her up. Like that's ever happening!" I sigh long and loud and shake my head in utter dismay.

Everything is starting to make more sense now. It's been ages since I got that last email from our nanny, my 'sister friend'. And I got so caught up in my own life that I haven't bothered reaching out to her anymore over the last few weeks. Figured she was too busy to keep in touch. Hah, she was busy alright. Messing up our lives forever. But of course, it works both ways. Our dad is just as guilty as she is of the same crime.

"And no wonder Dhanu gave Mom that ring," my brother says in a dazed voice. "She was probably doing her best to distract her. She knew Mom was obsessed with it. Always trying it on. Pretending like she was going to keep it."

"No kidding. So, it made her look like a hero by faking a big sacrifice. Why would Mom even suspect anything, especially with that 'magical' ring on her finger? That's some pretty vile magic. It magically made Dad completely screw up the rest of our lives. And totally destroy our mother's. Last time he did this she wound up in the hospital."

"I know," Jonah murmurs. "And I can't stop thinking about that. I mean, what if it happens again? What if we have to drop her off at that freaky psyche ward again?"

"Well, it's not freaky. It's in a hospital. You realize that place actually helped her, right? She came out a lot better than she was when she went in. Besides, we were way younger then. Maybe we can find a way to help her out this time. Look Jonah, we need to find a way to break it gently to her somehow, before she finds out herself."

Now I totally hate that stupid moonstone ring. And everything it represents. I hope I never even find it. That cursed thing needs to be gone for good. My brother's face is still as pale as chalk. He's still chewing, but on the skin around his thumb now. Chewing like he means business.

"Please don't gnaw your thumb off, okay?" I say, trying to be funny. He doesn't laugh.

"So how are we going to do it, Sophie," he murmurs in a ragged voice. "I hate that this is happening. It feels...it feels almost like someone died, you know."

I blink back a prickle of tears as I slide my arm around Jonah's shoulder.

"Let me think about this, okay," I tell him. "Try to stay calm. Try not to panic. And I know what you mean. It really does feel that way. Because this changes everything. As far as our lives go and as far as everything we've ever believed about Dhanu. And our own father. They've been living a lie. We're collateral damage. And now we have to do our best to help Mom survive."

Chapter Four

Tara

Behind me, I hear Mom's quick footsteps, feel her hand on my arm, gripping tightly. With a hard yank I pull myself loose and step outside into fading sunlight and cool air. Suck in a deep breath to help calm myself down a little before this inevitable confrontation.

"I'll be right back, Dave," she calls over her shoulder, then follows me out.

"That was incredibly rude, Tara Watson." Her nostrils are flaring, she's that mad. And I can see the hot red circles on her cheeks.

"You told him," I mouth to her so he won't hear. "Why! How could you do that after all the warnings you gave me about not blabbing to anyone."

She shrugs. "He doesn't need my money. He has his own money. He's a successful business man. And unlike me, great with finances, apparently, and I trust him."

"Yeah, right. Trust him? You hardly even know him! Did he tell you all that before or after you told him you won seventy-five grand? You're so freaking gullible. You believe every guy, until something crappy happens and you discover he's a total creep. And it all started with Dad."

I can't even looking at her now. She seems so happy with herself. Smug even. And I'm feeling nothing more than miserable about this new turn of events.

"Well, I have a good feeling about this one," she tells me with conviction. And a smile.

"Whatever, Mom. And even though you didn't ask, I have a bad feeling about it." I say as I turn around and walk away, reveling in the hurt look that melts away her smile.

Already I don't like the direction this new adventure of ours is headed.

* * *

I spot the first sign on my way to Starbucks. It's stapled to a lamp post, just as Priya predicted.

$$$ LOST / REWARD $$$

MOONSTONE RING WITH TWO DIAMONDS

SENTIMENTAL VALUE

And at the bottom there's a fringe of phone numbers with one torn off already. My heart takes a little flip-flop flutter. Clearly someone is missing their ring! And why wouldn't they be? I can barely stand not having it to look at, and it isn't even mine. It's such a pretty glittery distraction, too. There's no denying that I already feel a twang of guilt about not turning it in. But I'm still not quite ready to part with the ring yet, or certain how I should go about doing it.

What if I went to the police station and showed it to them? Promised I would keep it safe until the owner shows up. Or what if I asked them if anyone has reported a missing ring, because I heard something at school and I might know who lost it? Then I could leave them my cell phone number, and never risk Mom answering the phone if they call.

At least that way I could have it in my possession a little longer. Because the truth is, ever since I found it, circumstances have shifted in my life. Everything has suddenly turned upside down, it seems. Nothing is the same anymore. And I'm not quite ready to part with all the possibilities that the possibly charmed moonstone ring might be promising. The one that I'm carrying in my pocket right now, reminding me with its small hard bulge.

That's why I gather the courage to do the next crazy thing. I make sure nobody is watching, then tear the sign off the post and stuff it into my backpack. Then I start hunting for more. I find three of them in the neighbourhood and tear down every single one. After that I head for Starbucks with a bit of a sick feeling in my gut, but also an overwhelming sense of triumph that helps to ease it. Nobody will ever know the difference. And now, at least, I can still hang onto that ring for a while longer.

And nope, not proud of myself for doing it. I need to bury this feeling though, before it swallows me whole. Besides, I know that in the end I'll eventually have to give it up. Right now just isn't the right time. I still have too much thinking and planning to do.

I push through the glass door. The coffee shop is already crowded with kids our age, hunched over tables, scrolling through their phones while sitting with their friends, which is something I can finally do now if I want to. Kids I know from school are here, and tonight some unfamiliar kids. It's more crowded than ever for some reason. Luckily Priya has snagged a table. She's sitting with a guy, but I can see only the back of him. I hurry right over and pull up a chair.

"Sorry I'm late Priya. My mom's gross new boyfriend showed up and..."

Oh no. Silas is sitting at the table grinning at me. I feel as if all my bones have turned to spaghetti noodles. Silas showed up? Why would he even do that? A blush starts creeping up my neck and settles on my cheeks. I can't even imagine what my friend Priya is thinking right now.

"I figured I'd find you here," he says. "I was hoping that maybe the three of us can rehearse together." Uh oh. Momentary scary glare from my friend. And then...

"Oh, so *that's* why you're here." Priya's voice sounds almost like a low threatening growl. And her face has morphed from gleaming smile to deep frown in seconds flat.

By then I have a pretty good idea what she's thinking, and my heart instantly sinks. This is not going to turn out well.

"So, you already knew Tara was coming here tonight, huh Silas?" she says to him in a clipped voice. "Seems you both forgot to mention that."

When she turns to stare hard at me again, my face starts to burn. I look back at him.

Silas is still looking at me with that sweet sideways smile, completely guileless. Can't he figure out what's happening right now, how upset Priya is because she's got the wrong idea about his reasons for showing up here? I can't tear my eyes away from his heart-stopping face though, no matter how bad it might look to Priya right now. Totally mesmerizing, like the ring.

"Kind of took a wild guess. When I talked to Tara last night, she told me that you two are running though lines tonight. And everyone chills here on Saturday night, right?"

Uh-oh. I'm pretty sure Priya actually believes that Silas came here looking for *her*. Does she really think he might have a crush on her, when he only came here to rehearse with me? Oh, but it's becoming all too obvious now. Nasty vibes are already radiating from my friend. Her dark eyes have gone hard and cold. Her nostrils are flaring.

"How about that," Priya says with mock cheer in her voice. "I guess it's your lucky day again, isn't it, Tara?" Then she holds out her hand. Between her fingers there's a thin scrap of paper. With a phone number on it. "Look what I found. Thought you might need it. Lucky huh!"

Oh crap. So, she was the one who tore off the number from the sign? I take the scrap and play dumb, tilting my head in an 'I'm curious' way. Trying to pretend that I'm completely confused right now. "So, what is this about anyway?"

"Didn't you see the signs on the lamp posts on your way over here?" Priya asks with narrowed eyes. "You couldn't have missed them. They're right along your route."

"What signs? What are you talking about?" If ever I needed to use my scant acting skills, now is the time. I'm nailing this role right now.

"Just call the number, Tara. I'm sure you're smart enough to figure it out. So, are we rehearsing or what?"

Her voice is all snappy and impatient. I can tell that she's barely hanging on to her simmering anger. I've never seen this side of my best friend before, and it's kind of scaring the crap out me.

Silas is staring at both of us, looking totally confused. "What is happening," he says. "Am I totally missing something, or what?"

"You're asking the wrong person, Silas," Priya says with a weak smile. Then she squints at me, her face in a half sneer. If looks could kill. "Let's get started. I won't be staying too long. Gotta be someplace else in a while."

By the sullen look she can't disguise, she's lying. Anyplace else but here, is what she really means. She can't possibly believe that he came here looking for me because he likes me or something? Can she? We make a bit of small talk about the play, and how nice the sets are coming along, but clearly Priya's heart isn't in it at all.

And then Silas starts on something that sounds like a soliloquy about himself. Rambling on about plays he's starred in and his improv classes or something. Starts blathering about *Our Town*, and I think I hear my name come up, but I can barely even focus because of Priya. She won't even look my way, just sits there wearing a stony face. Then, before I'm halfway through my chai latte, before we've even begun rehearsing, she stands up and pushes out her chair, cutting him off mid-sentence.

"Okay, I'm done here," Priya says, leveling a steely gaze at me. "Catch you guys later. And make that call, Tara." Then she strides right out the door without even looking back.

Ugh. Awkward. Silas didn't even glanced at Priya once the whole time. But a few seconds ago, he started telling me how great I would be as Emily Webb, if by some fluke I need to step in as the understudy. How he figures that by now I must be starting to recite the lines in my sleep. I know darn well it's just wishful thinking. It's only because he wants to be sure I get it right, so he won't look like a fool on stage, that he's heaping praise on me. He ignored my friend completely. And I could tell that Priya was missing the point. It makes me feel awful. So as soon as she's gone, I just have to ask

"So, what's going on anyway, Silas? Why did you totally ignore Priya? She's my best friend, you know. And I think she's major upset right now."

"Did I?" he says, looking surprised. "Honestly, I didn't even notice."

Probably because he likes hearing the sound of his own voice too much. Hmm. I'm not too crazy about this self-centered side of Silas that he just revealed to us. I'm also kind of glad that my brief infatuation with this guy suddenly just shriveled up like a dead worm in the sun. Poor Priya. She has a bad crush on the wrong guy.

"Yeah, well I noticed, and you can bet that she sure did. You have to think about other people sometimes, you know. Try to be a little more considerate."

Woah! Did I really say that out loud? I must have because he's staring at me like I've slapped him. And I almost regret what I've just said, wish I could get a do-over of the last couple of minutes. The two of us have to work well together, just in case I need to fill in. And now I might have gone and ruined any chance of a good outcome.

I sit there, wide-eyed, doubting my intentions and waiting for his response. He stays silent for a moment, frowning a little, which makes me more nervous than ever.

"Geez, Tara, I honestly didn't mean to upset Prina, you know," he finally says. "I didn't do it on purpose. I just really get into my acting roles. I want to make sure I get it right."

"Don't you mean you want to make sure that *I* get it right?" I roll my eyes. Is this guy for real? "Her name is actually Priya, by the way. So, let's get to work and go over our lines now, okay? I wouldn't want to screw up your chances at winning an Oscar."

"You mean a Tony, right. Broadway equivalent of an Oscar award." Smug grin and wink. "I'm actually aiming for an EGOT designation someday. By winning an Emmy, Grammy, Oscar and Tony. The big four."

Seriously? "Whatever, dude," I tell him, rolling my eyes yet again.

I figure people don't try and boss Silas around every day. After all, just looking at him is almost intimidating. For me at least. But now I've seen another side of him, an arrogant one that's a bit of a turnoff. And for some reason that gives me courage. Just defending my friend makes me feel more self-assured. Maybe if I have to step into the Emily role opposite Silas Symonds, I really can pull it off after all.

So that's what we do for the next little while. Sit across from each other and shoot lines back and forth. And I can't deny that I'm proud of the fact that I'm sitting with him, at first. The way everyone around me is reacting tells the story. They're all texting each other as they watch us, and probably sending messages to all their friends.

You'll never guess who Tara is sitting with…

Silas is here with Tara! OMG…

Did you have any idea about these two…

And so on, and so on, blah blah blah. I know for a fact that I've never been the subject of viral text messaging before now. And deep down I kind of like that feeling. Boring little old me, finally becoming the object of envy among the other girls. I am owning this one, and I work hard at faking pleasure in his presence. After all, it can't look like I don't want to be here.

But after going over the lines a few times, it starts to get repetitive. I'm actually having trouble concentrating, because by then, all I can think about is Priya and how hurt she might be. I keep seeing the shock and dismay in her eyes, and the way her face fell when she figured out that he wasn't here to see her. Her disappointment morphing to simmering anger, and the way she fled the coffee shop not long after I arrived, clearly utterly crushed. Then I start flubbing my lines, even though I know them really well at this point. Silas keeps glaring at me across the table. I can see tables of others watching us, and my crazy imagination sees them as judging me. As if I shouldn't even be sitting at a table with this guy. As if I don't deserve the honour. It's making me more and more uncomfortable every minute.

"Hey, Silas," I finally say when I just can't handle the pressure anymore. "It's kind of getting late. I really need to get home, or my mom will start to get worried."

"Seriously?" he says. "It's not even ten o'clock yet. And tomorrow is Sunday."

"Yes, seriously. My mom will worry about me." I half glare at him, and half wonder if my mom will even be home from her date night yet.

And Silas actually seems shocked that a girl is giving him the brush off instead of the other way around. It probably doesn't happen to him often. I just leave him there, sitting at the table with a fresh cappuccino, looking surprised. And I'm surprised at how good that feels.

As soon as I'm out the door, I start texting Priya.

Please let me explain!!!! Please call me, Priya!!!!

But she never replies. I hate how this has happened between us. My best friend has been left feeling disappointed and betrayed just because of a misunderstanding. Ever since I've known her we've been like two peas in a pod. And now this awfulness that has left me feeling like I've been socked in the stomach. I feel all knotted up inside.

How has a simple situation like being in a play suddenly become so complicated?

Once I'm home, thoughts of my possibly lost friendship keep cluttering up my positivity as I try to enjoy the relaxing solitude while Mom is still out on her date. I do my best to banish my guilt over Priya, distracting myself by staring at the ring instead, stroking the smooth curve of the pale stone. And wondering about other things instead.

Like how did I ever summon the nerve to speak that way to Silas, the coolest guy in our drama troupe? Why do I suddenly have so much more courage and confidence these days? Why do I feel as if nothing can stop me now? Is this magnificent ring really working in my favour, or simply a figment of my overactive imagination, and wishful thinking?

On my smart phone I Google moonstone properties yet again. And everything I read points that way. 'Inner strength', 'emotional growth', 'self-awareness'. Qualities I always thought I lacked, and now I'm practically brimming with them. So, I need the ring for at least a few more days, because of the super-charged way it helps me feel, as though it really is my lucky charm. No denying I'm still extremely curious about what might happen next. And based on the mostly awesome way things have been going since I found it, how can I possibly give it up now?

Which is why I retrieve the crumpled lamp post signs from my backpack, tear each one up into tiny pieces, and flush them down the toilet, along with my swelling sense of guilt. All I need is a reminder of how I've possibly made a bad choice. Which I really haven't, after all, since I'm obviously going to turn the ring in eventually. As soon as I find a chance, since what with the play and Priya and Silas, plus school work and my mom's angst, there's just so much other stuff cluttering up my best intentions right now. And honestly, just looking at this ring helps to boost my mood and make me feel more positive about everything else. So instead of wallowing in guilt and self-pity, I lie on my bed watching Youtube videos on my phone 'til I hear the key in the front door near midnight.

A minute later, Mom flings open my door and sticks her head in my bedroom.

"It's official! I'm in lo-ove!" she sings. "I'm telling you, he's the real deal!"

I groan and whip my covers up over my head. This is one of the many things cluttering up my life right now and making me crazy. This new guy of Mom's is hanging over me like a heavy blanket of fog, threatening to envelop me any minute. As much as I've been trying to push it to the back of my mind, it's still there, suffocating all of my almost happiness. Why does she keep doing this to me, and to herself? Can't she find an easier way to be content with life, instead of a more complicated one?

"Oh wow. Yay for you, Mom," I mutter through the sheets. "I hope you and Prince Charming live happily ever after."

All I hear is my mom laughing in a breezy way as she closes my bedroom door. It's a rosy hopeful sound that I haven't heard in ages, if ever. And a sound that I'm not sure I will ever get used to hearing because it doesn't sound like my real mom at all. In fact, it sounds like a complete stranger, as if someone I've never even met has moved into the house with me.

After that it's hard to fall asleep. And I can't deny it anymore. As much as I want to believe that this ring is changing my life in a good way, there's a whisper of new doubt in my subconscious. Suddenly nothing is the way it used to be. Everything seems to have turned upside down. And I don't know if that's a good thing or a bad one.

The word I keep hearing in the back of my mind is *bogus*. And that's probably because I'm not even sure what is real anymore. In my own life as well as my mom's.

*** *

Sophie

I'm so obsessed and distressed by Dad's latest awful deception that I can't even concentrate for the rest of the day. How could he have even done something so atrocious to our family? Now I realize that I never should have forgiven him for what happened last time he cheated on Mom. Or trusted him either. And I'm not sure that I even want to see him again. Worst father ever.

Over a grilled cheese lunch Jonah is silent, taking small nibbles of the sandwich instead of his usual huge bites. He still looks completely dazed too. I'm actually more worried about him now than I am about Mom. At least our mom is on stabilizing meds for her anxiety and depression. But today she's been unusually chirpy, which can be scary with her cyclothymia, a milder form of bipolar. She almost seems on the verge of manic. Jonah has to suffer in silence and he's likely aching to the core. He wants us to be a family and stay a family. I'm so used to hearing about broken relationships at school, though, that I realize sometimes the best option is for parents not to stay together for the sake of the kids. Because sometimes that can screw them up even more.

Leaving half the sandwich on his plate, my brother quietly drifts up the stairs to his room, and I'm left to tidy up and wonder and worry about his troubling silence. Then a while later, when I'm trying to set aside my family angst long enough to get some work done so I won't feel guilty when I go out tonight, I get a text from Lexi.

Guess what! We cant go to Timothys tonight

What! WHY!

Cuz its CLOSED! For renovations. Just saw the sign in the window

Oh no. So now what

Starbucks I guess. With the riff raff bourgeoisie. I'll let everyone know and go early to grab a good table. Later.

Kk cya.

Riff raff bourgeoisie. That's what she calls the public school kids. She can be such a bitch sometimes. Honestly we're all just a bunch of dopey kids. Trying our best to survive the horrors of high school. Just trying to keep it all together, too many balls in the air, juggling madly. Yup I'm still cynical. No doubt about that.

* * *

Throughout the rest of the afternoon, I avoid leaving my room. I don't feel like talking to Mom, who is in her room 'purging

98

her stuff' as she describes it. She's now glommed onto that trend where you free yourself from too many possessions by only keeping the ones that spark joy. Mom has a lot of work to do. And I'm not sure that anything sparks joy in her life.

Or if anything ever even will.

The good thing about my room is that it looks down on basketball boy's driveway. He's out there bouncing while I'm sitting at my desk. And even though he claimed yesterday that the bouncing keeps him focused and helps him to concentrate, it's having the total opposite effect on me right now. Bounce bounce bounce clang, ball through the hoop. On and on and on.

I crouch on my window seat to watch for a while. It's sure easy to fixate on his perfect body in action. 'Poetry in motion'. I think that's a saying isn't it? I google it on my phone and yup that just about describes him perfectly. Pleasing to all five senses. Well, I'm hoping to find out for sure about that. He's easy on the eyes though, and his voice is rich and deep. Maybe soon I'll even be close enough to touch him and smell him. Oh, and taste him, yummy. Sigh. I actually sneak a couple of photos, then immediately delete them because 'stalking'!

What a loser, Sophie. Get back to work. Finish the damned essay. But it's still there. Nonstop. Bounce bounce bounce, clang. Ack! Driving me to distraction with every single never-ending bounce and clang.

The knock on my bedroom door is almost welcome. Until it swings open, and Mom is standing there with her beautiful silky chocolate milk-stained cream top in her hands. Why does that stain look so much darker now than it did yesterday?

"Keep or let go?" she says, frowning deeply. "Let go, I think. Because I can't see any more joy in my favourite top. Can you? Because you did this, didn't you?"

Poor Mom. Getting all upset about the stupid top, when she has no clue what's really going on in her life. If I told her right now, she'd completely forget about that stupid stain.

"Oh, and I still can't find that ring anywhere. It's so bizarre. I've searched high and low in this house. I've looked in my car. I'd really love to find it. In fact, I really need to find it. Ever since I put it on, everything has changed. It's the strangest thing, you know. I've just been feeling so..."

Uh-oh. She might be starting to spiral toward another crash. Distraction tactic alert.

"Oh Mom, I'm so sorry about your top. Yes, it was totally my fault. I spilled chocolate milk on it. I was out on the porch trying to flirt with the hot new guy next door. And I took a sip of the milk, it was totally gross, and I spurted it out all over your top. And I was pretending to read so he'd think I'm smart, but I accidentally pulled the wrong book off the shelf. *Fifty Shades*! Can you even believe it? Imagine what he was thinking. So anyway, I bet if I try soaking that and using some stain remover, it will come clean again. Want me to try?" I slap a very deliberate look of sadness and regret on my face, hoping she'll forget about the stupid ring. "Honestly can you ever forgive me?"

But the shocking thing is, Mom has started laughing. Her whole face has changed. She's laughing so hard, she's bent right over. I haven't seen her laugh this hard in ages. This could be a very good thing or a colossally bad thing.

"Wow! Massive fail," she gulps out between bouts of hysterical laughter. Hmm.

"Well, I'm glad you think I was a complete idiot too," I tell her, feeling suddenly a little bit defensive about my stupid moves with basketball boy.

"Oh Sophie, it's not that. It's just that it all seems so absurd. Like a scene from a silly rom-com or something. You really shouldn't have to go through so much trouble to get a guy's attention. Honestly. You're trying way too hard. And don't worry about the top. I have another one in a very pale lilac which I love even more. Don't lay a hand on it, though. Promise?"

"Oh, thank God. Sorry Mom, seriously I'm so sorry."

"No worries. And hey, why don't you just walk right up to him and say hi Silas? Oh, his name is Silas, by the way. I met him the other day. He's eye candy, alright!" She throws the top at me and I catch it in midair. "It's all yours now, Sophie. Good luck getting that stain out."

It's almost embarrassing that my mom beat me to the punch and found his name out before I even did. But my ploy actually worked, and she didn't mention the ring again after I cracked her up with all my ridiculous fails yesterday.

Silas, Silas, Silas. It's like music to my ears. I remember liking that name when we studied that boring George Eliot novel *Silas Marner* last year. Now that I know his name, I'm even more fixated on the thought of him. And that ball bouncing in the driveway keeps on reminding me how close he is. Not in a really good way though.

After a while it starts bugging me so much that I have to move to the spare bedroom, Dhanu's room ugh, on the other side of the house so that I can concentrate. But this two-thousand word essay on Buddhism versus Hinduism, and which I would choose if I wanted to embrace one of them, plus my reasons why, is making me a bit crazy. Why would our World Religion teacher Ms. Martino even assign something like that, where we actually have to think and analyze, instead of just digging through the internet for facts. Like she actually wants us to waste too much time thinking about this.

Sadly, I manage only three bad paragraphs before Mom calls us for supper. I do think I'm leaning towards Buddhism, though. I like the idea of meditation for salvation. It seems way easier than all those Hindu rituals and random gods. But as far as my daily actions and thoughts go, I'd sure have a lot of work to do in order to be saved. Which actually made me stop typing for a few minutes and rethink some of the choices I've made lately. Ugh. Self-guilt trip.

I hear Jonah thumping down the stairs ahead of me as usual. So, I make sure I save my essay document by emailing it to myself, then check that it's landed in my inbox. Then I scroll back to a month-old email from Dhanu which I'd saved before I knew the truth. I click on it right away to see how well she was carrying on the deception that we've just unearthed.

Hi sister friend, how are things over there? I hope all is well. I'm okay over here. My amma is doing better and I'm so happy about that. I miss you all so much though. How is everyone doing? I think about you every day. I hope your mom has been able to find someone to take over some of my daily upkeep for her. And I hope your dad doesn't miss me over-starching his shirts ha ha. Is Jonah still eating you out of house and home? Once amma has recovered, I hope to be able to come back and visit you at your lovely home in Toronto again. It was such a wonderful way for me to improve my English and to find a whole new family to love.

Wow seriously! Now that I know what's been going on with Dhanu and Dad, her old message is just a huge dung pile of irony. Delete! I have to try and erase the thought of her from my brain, because I still feel so deceived and duped. Was she a scammer all along? A crushing thought, since I loved her so much. Has she done this before? Is she going to try and get money out of Dad and then just ghost him? Ugh, I need to stop thinking about this. Checking out Mom's latest attempt at cooking will be a start. So will hanging out with my friends at Starbucks tonight.

* * *

By the time I dash out my door in the direction of the local Starbucks, I'm feeling a bit overstuffed. The jog will do me good after the giant chow down on a delicious dinner. Zucchini stuffed with ricotta and spinach and baked like a lasagna? Where did she come up with that one? When I asked her at dinner she winked at me and smiled and said she's trying lots of new things. She's been full of surprises lately, which is weird for our mom.

When I reach the bus stop corner near the local coffee shops, I suddenly remember the signs I put up. I wonder if anyone has ripped off one of the little phone number flaps. Because my mom is still so fixated on that ring, I need to get it back pronto and hide it where she can find it in our house. But something strange is afoot. On every single pole I check, every sign is missing.

So, what should I do now? Ask Jonah to print off some new ones and try again. Why would someone rip down those sign? Because they found that expensive ring and they don't want to give it up, I bet. I guess that makes the most sense in this whole thing. Finders keepers?

I'm still trying to make sense of it when I walk into Starbucks and start scanning the room. This would have been our java shop of choice if the other kids hadn't chosen it first. Lexi isn't into the public school kids, and her opinions are the opinions of choice in our friend circle. Sadly. I wish I could have more influence over the other sheep. But I'm one too, I guess. I still can't figure out how Lexi has so much power over all of us. And there they are, in a primo fireplace spot. She must have gotten here really early. But OMG, who's that a couple of tables over but freaking Silas. As soon as she sees me, Lexi's eyes grow wide and so does her grin.

"About time," she hisses as I drop into a chair feeling gobsmacked with dismay.

"OMG," is all I can whisper. "Why didn't you text me. At least I would have tried harder with my clothing choices. God, Lexi!"

My skinny jeans are too loose and need re-shrinking. My grey school hoodie has pasta sauce on one cuff. Jeez. I nonchalantly try licking it off and it tastes super gross. Might even be an old stain. Lexi's dressed like she's going clubbing, of course. She crouches beside me before I can stop her, then takes a selfie and posts it. Ugh. I can't wait to see what she hash-tagged.

"Because I wanted to surprise you, babe, lol," she tells me, when she looks up from her screen. Our other three friends laugh on demand like trained seals. Just the way Lexi likes it. And I'm pretty sure she didn't bother to warn me about Silas, just to make me look bad. Typical Lexi move.

"Would have appreciated the heads up instead," I grumble, as I side-eye Silas.

He's sitting there with a couple of girls. And I don't know if I'm feeling envious, or furious or curious, or a little of all three. There seems to be an awkward silence. As well as some pretty nasty body language happening between the two girls. One of them just handed something to the other one. Too small to see. The other girl looks mortified.

"Got you a grande low fat almond milk latte like you always order." Lexi pushes it over. "Hello in there. Quit staring Soph! You're so obvious." She waves her hand in front of my face, so annoying.

"Shut up, Lex," I growl at her, then smile on the inside when her face sags. Then I keep right on staring because I need to figure out what's happening, if there's some sort of rivalry going on. What chance do I stand against either of these two anyway?

I sip my latte and try to pay attention to my four friends, but it's just the usual boring blather about guys they're crushing on and girls they despise, and latest online purchases and which celeb is trending on TikTok today. I'm still watching the little ongoing drama, because it feels like a train wreck in the making. And I can't tear my eyes away. So, are these girls both crushing on Silas or what? Are they best friends, enemies or frenemies?

Suddenly the dark exotic beauty with a waterfall of black hair leaps to her feet.

"Okay I'm done here. Catch you guys later," she snarls so that too many ears can hear.

And then she heads straight for the door without looking back. Silas and the other girl, with soft brown curls that just reach her shoulders and a wide-open pretty face, just sort of look bewildered. Right after that, it sounds as though they're practicing something. Maybe lines from a play judging from booklets in their hands. Then the light goes on! Wow maybe that's what he's doing while he's bouncing that ball. It helps him concentrate on learning his lines or something. Hmm that sort of makes sense.

"Wake up, Sophie," Lexi snaps beside my ear. All four of them are staring at me.

"Wow, okay, sorry you guys," I tell them. "What were we just talking about?"

"*You*," Lexi says. "I was just telling the girls how you blew it after school yesterday. See what happens when you wait too long." She tilts her head toward Silas and the girl.

"Well, I still have an advantage. He lives right next door to me. So I can actually watch him in the driveway from my bedroom window. And I think maybe his bedroom window even faces mine."

"Perfect!" Lexi smiles in a thoughtful way. "You could flash him. Press your boobs against your window and knock until he looks up. That's what I'd do anyway. You have zero finesse with these things, you know. Listen and learn."

Grrr. Why is she pressing my buttons right now? "Yeah, well you always make really great choices, huh Lex," I remind her. "Like that time you decided to drunk streak the party at Joshua's house and ran straight into his parents out in their driveway. That was a classic!"

The trained seals don't know whether to laugh or gasp about her brutal faux pas that brought the party to a crashing halt. They all turn to wait for Lexi's reaction. Her face looks pretty somber, until she cracks right up. Then they all do as well.

"That was epic," she half shrieks, then starts to laugh way too loud.

But then her face turns cold and harsh like a vicious switch just turned on in her brain.

"The sad truth, Sophie, is that you haven't made out with anyone since what, last year, when you went out with that dweeb Atticus from Saint Barnabas downtown. Who none of us even met. And who I have my doubts even existed—did you, like, find his photo online? I mean, dude seriously, that relationship lasted about ten minutes, didn't it? Speaking of great choices."

"Oh snap, Lexi," says one of our friends.

The others just stare at me, waiting for my comeback. Atticus broke my heart. He was a total player, I sadly learned. It took me months to get over him and I suffered in silence. I smile in a pseudo calm way, take a deep breath. Bite back my fury.

"You know what's great about having you as a friend, Lex," I say, speaking slowly and forcing a bright smile. "Almost every day you provide another lesson for us on how to behave like an odious and tawdry human being! We listen and we learn. And I can't thank you enough!"

Long deliberate pause and a frown as Lexi mulls these words over. Then her eyes open wide. Uh oh. Maybe that was a little too harsh? But then, wow, her face explodes into a glad and rapturous smile, as do the faces of the rest of her fans at our table, right on cue.

"Sophie, that's probably one of the nicest things anyone has ever said to me. You know

I always try my best to help people, right?" The rest of them nod on cue. "I just do what I do, and somehow it all works out." She checks out her manicure, then looks at us again.

"Well, yay for you," I tell her with joy in my voice.

Do they even realize that I just dissed the hell out of her, Lexi and the grinning rest of them? I mean, she either thinks I'm joking, or thinks I'm perfectly serious and has no clue what I just said. And I don't know which is worse. How can I stay mad at a girl this egotistic and clueless when every day I'm inevitably entertained? Actually, she's kinda right. I do lack finesse with these things. And I just keep right on reporting in to her.

And then suddenly there's a commotion nearby, and the other girl at Silas's table is on her feet. She stares down at him and says something in a low voice, and then she's gone, out the door into the April twilight and he's left just sitting there in shock, scraping his fingers through his thick dark hair.

"Now's your chance, doofus," Lexi says, nudging me with her sparkly platform sneaker. "Go for it, Soph. Because if you don't, then I will. Dude is majorly hot. Oh, just face it. You have zero guts. Guess I have to help you out with this, as usual." Exaggerated eyeroll and head shake.

Grr. She makes me so crazy! I pick up my latte and stroll right on over to his table.

"Hey, Silas," I say. "You need help going over those lines?"

"Wait, what?" he says, gorgeous dark eyes so confused. "How did you even know..."

Then I do it. Sit right down in the chair across from Silas that the other girl just ditched. And smile super wide. Over at Lexi's table, every mouth is hanging half open. Especially hers.

Zero guts? Hah!

Chapter Five

Tara

On Sunday morning I wake up late to voices in the kitchen, the aroma of frying bacon and fresh coffee, and teaspoons stirring cream and sugar into coffee mugs. All very unusual sounds for our place, where my depressed mom usually sleeps in later than me.

Oh please! Not Dave here already. But then I hear Lyla's loud and frantic voice. It's the way she always sounds, over enthusiastic about every little thing. Her loud voice bounces off the walls of our ugly little house, rattling my barely-awake brain. I pull on my robe and shuffle barefoot down the hall, where I stop in the doorway and purposely yawn wide and loud.

"Well! Good afternoon," Mom says. "Gosh Tara, it's nearly eleven. Lyla popped by to have brunch with us and celebrate. I'm making French toast too."

"Well how about that, Mom. You actually got out of bed before me for a change," I say, and she offers me a withering smile. "Hey, Lyla. How's it going anyway?"

"Never been better," she says. "How about that mom of yours and her big win. I hear you scratched the lucky ticket. So, is she giving you half or what?" She starts cackling hysterically.

I roll my eyes. "Yeah, like that's ever gonna happen. I wouldn't even know what to do with it anyway. But I got a phone out of the deal, which is awesome."

"Sweet, Tara. And actually, Marie," Lyla says to my mom in a more serious tone, "I have a few thoughts about that prize money. And what you could do with it. There are so many possibilities. It's like you have this chance to start a whole new chapter in your life."

I think the hairs actually prickle on the back of my neck.

"Huh. Like what kind of ideas, exactly, Lyla?" I ask with a touch of venom in my voice. "Something smart and rewarding, I hope."

Mom and Lyla both stare at me with the same look of astonishment. I sit there quietly, blinking at them. I've never been very sassy with my mom. Maybe this is turning into a whole new chapter for me, too. After all, someone needs to dish out a reality check to Mom before she goes crazy and does something stupid with the money.

"What's that supposed to mean?" Mom says, waving a spatula in the air. "You think

I'm gonna make a bad choice? Because it sure sounds that way to me."

"I just don't want you to waste it, that's all. Or to lose it all doing something dumb. You haven't exactly made the best choices in the past."

When Mom's face drops and she stares at me long and hard, my stomach takes a dip.

"I find that a bit offensive," she almost snarls. "And if you're referring to your dad, I chose to leave. So that life would be better for the both of us. So tough luck, Tara. Things can't always go your way, you know."

Those words make me bristle even more. Everything is always about her. And so far, absolutely nothing better is in sight.

"When have they ever gone my way, Mom? Do you think I wanted you and Dad to have a crappy relationship then a nasty break up? Do you think I like living in this dump? If things were going my way, you'd actually have a job instead of just shopping online for a new guy. Who will never fulfill your ridiculous dreams!" As my rant winds down, I suck in a deep breath.

"Maybe I'd better leave," Lyla says, squirming in her chair.

Yes, please go, I can't help thinking. Right now, it feels as if Lyla is interfering in our problems, or whatever they are. And she needs to mind her own business, let Mom and me figure out a way to deal with this ourselves.

"No, stay here, Lyla. I'd love to hear some of your ideas. Maybe you'd better go, Tara. Go somewhere and think about everything you said just now."

Mom's face is hard as stone. I don't like the way she's looking at me, with something like fury. I've never seen her quite like this before. It doesn't look good on her either. Is this what happens when people win money? Does everything suddenly turn nasty?

"Gladly," I say then slap the doorframe hard with my hand before I turn to leave.

"Wait a sec," Mom says, and I turn back slowly to look at her. Maybe she's sorry suddenly. Maybe she can see my side of the story after all. "What's that on your finger?"

Crap. I look at the moonstone ring, which seems more luminescent than ever in the sun-bright kitchen. Big mistake, forgetting to take it off. I need to do some damage control, pronto. I shrug. Try to act all innocent. "Just some cheap thing I found."

"Doesn't look cheap," Lyla says, way too loud. "Looks like white gold to me."

"Let's see it," Mom says, taking a couple of steps toward me. I take a step back.

"Jeez, why don't you ever believe me, Mom? And why can't you just leave me alone, for God's sake," I snark. Then I stomp down the hall to my room and slam the door.

My hands are shaking. My body is actually trembling as my eyes fill with tears. What's wrong with me lately? Nothing feels the same anymore. My anger seems to be hair trigger, and I'm always on edge. And then the truth washes over me with a shiver of unease. The freaking moonstone hasn't changed me — I'm changing because of the ring.

Ever since I found it I've been feeling more confident, but I've grown bolder as well. And secretive and sneaky, too. Just so I can hang onto that stupid ring even longer. I've been making some questionable decisions lately. Hurting people for absolutely no reason. Now everyone seems to be turning on me, including my best friend. It's not just my mom who's changed. I'm turning into someone I don't even know anymore, becoming a stranger to myself.

Okay, now I need to get rid of this thing fast. But I don't want to hand it over to the police. That process feels too complicated, and might take ages to get resolved, if it ever even does. No, I want to drop that ring right into the hand of the person who lost it. To make certain that all its strange karma will stop rubbing off on me. And since I flushed away the little scrap with the phone number that Priya handed to me in Starbucks, I can't even make the call.

But one way or another I need to find whoever it was that put up the sign and give back the bedazzling moonstone ring that's clearly jinxed. Because my crow-like obsession with a sparkling object is affecting me in ways I never could have imagined. I'm half considering just putting it back where I originally found it and letting someone else deal with the problem. But that idea doesn't sit well with me. Now I almost feel a sense of obligation to the person who lost it. She needs to get that ring back.

And one way or another I have to get it out of my life for good.

* * *

Right after they've finished eating, Mom takes off somewhere with Lyla, doesn't even mention where she's going. And I don't even care. Because I have work to do that I don't want her finding out about. All I need is someone else besides Priya and my own guilty conscience nagging me to do the right thing.

After scarfing down cold French toast, I make new signs with a black marker.

!!RING FOUND!!

WOULD LIKE TO REUNITE IT WITH THE OWNER!!

PLEASE PROVIDE DETAILED DESCRIPTION

TO PROVE IT'S YOURS.

Along the bottom I carefully cut a few fringes, just like on the signs I tore up. And I write my cell phone number on each one. Ugh. Not exactly a work of art, and without a printer the signs look pretty lame, but this is the best I can do in a pinch. After that, I take off on my bike to tape them up on the same lamp posts where I found them yesterday. And then cross my fingers that the true owner of the moonstone ring will get in touch with me sooner than later.

Mom doesn't show up until nearly dinner time that evening. She brings in all the fixings for a steak dinner. Thick T-bone steaks, foil-wrapped potatoes, a huge container of mixed green salad, a crusty baguette. And a heaping apple pie for dessert. I stand in the doorway with my arms crossed, watching her happily humming as she unloads her grocery bags, and guilt wells up inside of me.

"What," she finally says, with the impatient gaze that I've been seeing far too often lately. "Did I waste my money on this meal? Or was it a 'smart and rewarding' choice?"

"I'm sorry, Mom," I murmur. "I'm kind of stressed out. I have a lot of understudy lines to learn for the play. The show is coming up fast."

Her face solemn, she sits down at the table. Then she pushes a chair toward me.

"We need to talk," she says. Those four words every kid dreads. I sit down, slowly.

"Oka-y-y-y," I say. "So, what's up?"

Mom reaches across the table, grabs my hand and launches right into her lecture. "We've been through some tough times. And I realize things haven't always worked out great. But you're older and more independent now, Tara. So, don't you think maybe, just maybe, it's my turn? To grab a chance at life? I've been trying my best for you, haven't I?"

I stare at the table, pretty sure Mom wouldn't want to hear my answer to her question. Because the truth is, I'm not totally convinced that she actually has tried her best. Sometimes I feel as if I'm always looking out for her feelings. And she never seems to be as concerned about mine. When I finally glance up, she has tears in her eyes.

"Okay, you don't have to answer that. And sure, I've been wrestling demons. I haven't often been pleasant to live with. But everything's changing now. I promise."

I've heard that line before too. "Whatever, Mom. Sometimes everything *never* changes. Not. One. Little. Bit."

A tear trickles down her cheek. "But everything happens for a reason, or so the saying goes. And these past couple of days have been crazy, as far as strange things happening too fast! So maybe this time things really will change."

Crazy and strange indeed. I squeeze her hand. "I hope you're right. This time," I tell her. "Now let's get to work on this amazing dinner. I'm freaking starved."

Mom brushes her tears away and her lips curl into a half smile. Can I truly trust her this time?

"This time I promise, Tara Bear," she whispers my childhood nickname. "And guess what? Dave will be here in about half an hour or so. I can't wait for you to get to know him better. He's such a sweet guy, honestly. I can't believe my luck."

I pull my hand away and shake my head as she works on a wobbly smile. So, this whole thing was a set up? She was just buttering me up so she could break the lousy news to me about Dave coming over? Some things never change at all, and probably never will. How do I manage to let her keep on manipulating me time and again? Why do I keep on falling for her obvious head games? Why haven't I learned after so many years?

"Call me when dinner's ready," I say, then spin around and head for my room.

* * *

I don't have much to say through that meal, but I watch them closely. Talk about mad body language. They sit across from each other, leaning in as if they're being drawn toward each other, even after such a short time. I might as well not even be sitting here. Dave asks me a few awkward questions about how I'm doing in school, and what my favourite subjects are. I give him one-word answers. Then he gives all his attention back to Mom.

As far as guys go, he isn't anyone's idea of a dream catch, the tall, dark and handsome Prince Charming of fairy tales. More like average height, a bit pale, a bit chunky, but with boyish good looks. He actually reminds me a bit of Sean Astin when he played in *Stranger Things*. Something is definitely different about my mom while she's sitting across from him, though. It's the first time in ages that she looks really pretty, with her light touch of make-up and dark, blow-dried hair. New faded jeans and a nice daffodil yellow sweater, too—she's been shopping. And a new light in her eyes. She smiles and laughs as they carry on, talking about their past bad dates, and the perils of on-line dating sites. She looks so honest-to-goodness happy.

Again, the word bogus nudges into my thoughts. Is this really for real? Please don't let her get hurt again. I just want her to be truly happy for real this time. But my negativity won't back off. Nothing has ever worked out well for us in the past. So why should it work out this time?

"Well, it was nice to meet you, Dave," I interrupt their bliss, making my exit as soon as I've polished off my dinner and rinsed my plate. "I have some homework due tomorrow."

"No apple pie, sweetie," Mom says, statement more than question. I'm sure she means it that way too. Don't stick around for apple pie, Tara. We want to be alone now.

"Maybe later, Mom. For a bedtime snack." I smile at her knowingly.

"So wonderful to meet you too, Tara," Dave says, extending his hand.

And by the earnest look in his blue eyes when we shake, I'm almost sure he means it. This is so not easy, I'm thinking as I head for my bedroom. Trying to figure out everything weird and abnormal that's suddenly happening in my life, trying to navigate the changes.

This whole experience feels like walking into a bizarre new world that I've never visited before. On some distant planet in a parallel universe where everything is the same, but different. I'm not sure how to act around Mom right now. I'm seeing a whole new side of her. Plus, I'm carrying around all the ring guilt right now too. Any wonder my moods are on a rollercoaster ride, just as much as Mom's are.

Whatever's going on these crazy days, whether good or bad, I know it's time to try and embrace the changes if I can and try my best to set my mind on hope.

But first I really need to get rid of this crazy ring.

***

Sophie

On Sunday morning I wake up with a smile on my face, probably for the first time this year. I just nestle in my bed, lost in some sort of blissful stupor, going over and over every divine moment from last night. Or was I just imagining everything? Was it simply wishful thinking? It sure didn't feel that way at the time. I mean, there were so many clues.

The way his face lit up when I boldly sat down at his table. How he so easily opened up to me about his dreams to be on the Broadway stage someday, after he conquers the Stratford and Shaw festivals up here in Canada. How we shared a chocolate brownie, and he let me have the last bite because he needs to watch his weight, which made us both crack up. How he kept talking about some guy named Damon, who's his biggest rival in his weekly improv class, and always seems to one-up him when it comes to getting the last laugh. How his favourite musical ever is *Hedwig* and the something or other, which I've never heard of, and how he'd love to play the lead someday. I even loved the faraway look in his coffee-coloured eyes each time he talked about everything important in his life. I'm actually glad he never asked me anything about myself. Right now, isn't such a good time for that. Right now, everything in my life except for the Silas part, is pretty much in tatters, and if he'd asked, I might have burst into tears. I don't even want to think about the huge family betrayal that's happened. All I want to think about is Silas.

The best part of all was how we walked home together after Starbucks. The best part was how Lexi and the girls were left at the table drooling over my big win last night. I barely even said goodbye to them after Silas and I spent an hour on the play called *Our Town*. I took the role of Emily, and he was George, and God how I was wishing that I could actually be playing that role opposite him, especially when they share their quick kiss during the wedding scene when the action freezes, which I would have totally dragged out. Sadly, that didn't happen.

At the end of our driveways, after a nice slow moonlit walk, and lots of shared laughter—especially after we talked about my massive fail when I was trying to introduce myself on Friday—Silas hugged me. Yes, he did. It was a really sweet hug, too, and he looked right into my eyes, and he said how much he enjoyed chilling with me, and hoped that maybe I'd be able to help him out again sometime in the near future. We even exchanged cell numbers. Perfect ending.

Which is why I'm finding it so hard to get out of bed this morning. I finally check my phone after lying there for way too long, postponing the essay I need to work on, and postponing showing my face in the kitchen, where Mom might start mentioning the ring again. There's a whole series of curious, then angry texts from Lexi. And I know why too. I could feel my phone vibrating in my pocket all the way home last night. And I didn't look once. Or even reply to her before bed. I knew exactly what was coming from that girl. Now, I stare at my screen, grinning.

What's going on S?

R U home yet?

Did you make out?

Why aren't u answering me?

Why r u being such a beeatch?

Okay I give up, beeatch. Going to bed now

Are u up yet!!! Call me girlfriend!!!

Okay so I guess maybe I should call her before she loses it. I love that I have her so intrigued. Usually, it's all about Lexi. This time it's all about me for a change. She answers on the first ring, of course.

"Why didn't you answer any of my texts? Why are you being so mysterious? Did he make a move on you? Did you make a move on him? Did he even..."

"Shut up for a sec," I tell her, and she actually does. I can almost hear her simmering anger crackling over the invisible cell phone waves. Or whatever they are. Lexi loves to be the one in charge, control freak that she is. It's just nice to know that she's frustrated with me this time instead of the other way around like always. "Nothing happened, okay?"

Silence for a count of three. Then: "You lie. I saw how he grinned up at you when you walked over to his table. He is so totally hot for you. I can tell, and I'm so-o-o-o freaking jelly. I mean, why didn't I think of doing what you did last night! How did I miss that!"

"He grinned because I offered to help him with something, you nerd. I saw that he had a script on the table when he was with the other girls. We talked some, then I helped him rehearse for this play that he has a lead in, called *Our Town*. Remember we saw it with the school? He wants to be a famous actor someday."

"Cool. Okay so, imagine you hooked up with him and you both moved to New York or L.A.? And I could totally come visit you? So then what? Did he kiss you? Did you let him feel you up?"

"Don't be stupid Lex. I told you, nothing happened. We walked home together, we had some laughs. Well, he hugged me. But that's it. Thanked me for helping him out. He does talk about himself, but lots of people do, right? He was a total gentleman."

"Huh. No hands or tongue? That's weird. He didn't mention having a girlfriend? Because maybe he does, right? And you could have totally made the first move yourself, you know."

This girl makes me utterly crazy sometimes. And really pisses me off too.

"Seriously, Lexi, it's not always about tongues or groping, you know. A guy can respect a girl, too. Guys aren't always looking for a quick way to hook up first thing. Relationships don't always start with making out."

"They don't?" she says, and she really is serious. "Hmm. That's not how it works with the guys I've been out with. As you already know." Lascivious snicker.

"In excruciating detail," I remind her. Which is totally gross and annoying, I don't say out loud. We've heard way too much about Lexi's so-called love life. "And anyway, I got the impression that he's seriously committed to his career, at all costs."

"Huh. Well, that was an epic bore," she says with a sigh. "Text me later if you talk to him again today or anything. And I'm telling you. Flash your boobs at the window. Do it, babe! Works every time." A suggestive wink. Oh Lexi.

"Bye," I say, then end the call.

Then it's back to Buddhism versus Hinduism. And I start to settle into that welcome essay daze that happens every time I start making serious headway on school essays. I need to be in the zone to get anything accomplished. I need to be staring at my screen, while the rest of the world around me is just a complete muffled blur. That's when my fingers start to fly, and that's where I am right now, and the word count is adding up and...

Bounce bounce bounce clang! Bounce bounce bounce clang!

Crap, this can't be happening right now. I practically leap across my room to the window, and I can see him down there, talking to himself as usual. Going over and over the words of his character George. He has no clue that I'm sitting up here looking out on him. And wow, that sound is the absolute worst, and I'd so love to slide my window up and yell 'stop it for the love of God' at the top of my lungs. But after making so much headway last night, I don't dare do it. He was so sweet last night. I don't want to screw up the progress I've already made. And I'm not one of those students that can slap on headphones and write essays to music. I need a pair of noise cancelling headphones, but we don't own any. Note to self. Ear plugs from drugstore, at least.

I sit at my desk again and try to focus. Even though I moved to the spare room last time, this is my bedroom. It's my sanctuary, where I'm most comfortable. My favourite place in the house. Everything I love is in this room. Even my first stuffed toy ever, a ratty rabbit with a worn out spot on the ear I always chewed on for comfort. I have a poster of my fave band, Arkells, and I have a poster of my fave superhero, Deadpool, because I'm secretly crushing on Ryan Reynolds. I have cool scarves draped over my lamps that I picked up at second hand shops, along with old framed paint-by-numbers, because they look so retro. And I even have a bookshelf stacked with all my favourite novels, like the Harry Potter and Narnia series which I've read more than once. And my awesome pillow-stuffed window seat for reading. Or spying on Silas, it would seem?

Just the thought of the spare room reminds me about Dhanu, which isn't a good thing right now. It's just a reminder that maybe Jonah and I should be sitting down to have a talk with Mom and expose Dad for the serial cheater that he truly is. Oh God, I can't even think about this right now. I need to talk to Jonah about our next step. But that bouncing is making me nutso! Is this how it's going to be forever. The family that just moved away this past winter hardly ever used the basketball hoop. Their kids were too young, and the odd time the dad would sink a few baskets. But now! It's only April. There's an entire summer of bouncing ahead. I may go mad.

My rambling reverie is suddenly interrupted by the sound of another male voice in the driveway.

"Hey, what took you so long, dude?" Silas's voice yells out.

Hmmm. Must investigate. I launch across the room to my window seat. And sure enough another guy is just climbing off his mountain bike. He's decked out in helmet and gloves and the spandex of a serious cyclist.

"Maybe the twenty kilometres I had to ride," his friend tells him as he takes off his helmet. "Just to visit you." They stand there grinning at each other, then high five.

"Seriously, good to see you again Zeke. I had my doubts about this ever happening. Thanks for texting me and making it so."

"Hey, it had to happen. So, let's see how quickly I whip your butt shooting hoops. Then I can help you rehearse. Because I know that's all you really want to be doing. You nailed the role of Jesus in *Jesus Christ Superstar* last year at Windgrove. Drama club kids are still traumatized that you left for another high school. Nice digs, by the way."

"Yeah, it's an okay house, I guess. Step up from my old 'hood. My new high school is okay, and there's a pretty good drama club, like I already told you. Okay, so let's do this."

When Silas fires the basketball at Zeke's head, he ducks just in time. Then the bouncing starts again, relentless and nerve-wracking. But I have a window seat and nope, not complaining right this second. Wow, this new guy is a stunner. I can clearly see his sparkly dark eyes from my window. And he has a curly crop of hair that makes me want to touch it. He's muscular and fit, and his dark skin is gleaming with a sweat sheen. Lexi would lose her mind. If she were here, she'd already be introducing herself and pushing for a date. I sit watching them as they pivot and spin and toss the ball. Wish

I had the guts to go out and join them. But no, that's just not me, I'm so not good at those things. That's when it hits me. And I start texting Lexi right away.

SOS!!! Get your butt over here pronto

Whats up S???

You'll see. Hurry cuz its epic. New guy next door

Another one??? Sweet! One each. I'll drive. omw

Lexi would never miss out on a chance to hang out since it beats studying or writing essays. The other problem with my old friend is that besides being a bit of a sex maniac, she's also a bit of a brainiac. Everything seems effortless for this girl. Sometimes she even has the time to help write papers for her friends. English, History, whatever. For money, of course or a sweet handbag. So even if she's in the middle of something right now, she'll drop it and jump in the car at the promise of an adventure. And she'll just stay up an extra hour or two tonight and whip off anything that's due tomorrow. Sure, she's got a ton of faults, especially being a major control freak, but she was right about one thing. She's awesome at stuff where I lack a certain finesse. She's finds a way of saying all the right things to guys, and I usually say all the awkward ones.

I've barely managed to type out a few more paragraphs when I hear a car door slam, so I peek outside through my front window that faces onto the street. Sure enough she's just pulled up in her folks' slick black Mercedes sedan. Mom is gone wherever, so Lexi is parked in our double driveway. And I can see her out there in a whisper of a dove grey slip dress and barely-there strappy heels, pretending to dig around in her back seat as she scopes out the eye candy playing ball in the driveway. Then she snatches up her Chanel handbag and gives them both a finger wave as she sashays up to our front door. I half trip over my feet in my rush down the stairs to meet her. I answer the door panting.

"Whew," she says as she steps inside. "It is major hot out there in the driveway, isn't it? How long were you going to keep this from me? So imagine we went out with them, and Silas got into acting in L.A. and I hooked up with that other guy, what's his name..."

"This just happened. And he's Zeke," I tell her, grinning as she expands her story.

"Nice name, okay, and Zeke and I go down there to chill with you. After I become a huge social media influencer, so I can afford to buy an awesome beach house. Maybe we can even be neighbours."

"You're even crazier than me," I tell her. "Since I've also been having some pretty insane daydreams about what might happen. Come on. Let's go up and watch them from my window."

We whip up the stairs, laughing our asses off all the way, then flop into the window seat to watch and drool over the smoke show down below.

"I'm not wearing a bra," Lexi says. "Perfect opportunity for a boob flash." Evil grin.

We crouch head to head and peer down. Beside the garage, the two guys are KISSING!

Chapter Six

Tara

In my room that evening, I start shifting my thoughts toward hope. Mostly, because I put up those signs, and could likely be rid of the ring soon. Maybe this ring really isn't a magical talisman. Maybe it's just been a matter of fate rather than luck. Maybe it was already written in the stars. Sure, Mom won money that I hope she'll use well. And she has a new guy now too, who isn't as awful as I expected. He seems to like her, and I can tell it's mutual. Right now, they're in the living room watching a movie. Maybe things truly are about to change for the better.

If only Priya would respond to my texts and calls, so I can straighten out the mess with Silas in Starbucks. And prove to her that I'm actively trying to find the owner of the ring, to restore her faith in me. Then maybe I'll be able to believe that a return to my nice new-normal life is on the horizon. But no such luck as much as I try time and again to reach her.

Before bed my stomach is grumbling for apple pie. But Mom and Dave are still out there. I can hear low murmurs as they chat. When I peek out of my bedroom, I realize the door is shut between the kitchen and the living room. Which means I could quite possibly sneak out and snatch a slice of pie without disturbing them.

I hustle down the hall, straight to the cupboard for a plate. Then stop dead when I hear four murmured words. '...the money you won.' I stop breathing. I need to hear the rest, and crouch there by the door, trying to pretend that I'm not spying on my mom by listening on the other side. That I'm only trying to protect her from herself and her bad choices. The ones that she seems to be making over and over again. What is her problem? Where's her good sense? Oh right, she never really had any to begin with! I feel a little sick to my stomach right now.

"I'm a bit nervous about doing that," Mom says. "I haven't known you very long. How can I be sure that..." Nuts, missed the rest of her sentence.

"...always a gamble," Dave tells her, and my heart picks up speed. What's a gamble? "But we've been getting closer for a couple of months now since we first connected. I think we've really clicked, don't you? I've been doing this a long time, Marie. You can trust me."

Seriously? Long thick pause. Are they kissing now? 'Please don't do this, Mom,' I yell inside my head. I would love to just burst into the room and start yelling NO STOP MOM, but that probably wouldn't go over very well.

"But I haven't had money for a long time, you know. More like never," Mom says. "So, I'm new at this. And pretty clueless."

She sure got that one right. My sudden new hope is already starting to fizzle away.

"Don't worry. I'll guide you through the whole thing. It's a simple enough process. You just have to make a bank transfer to..."

My brain is screaming STOP! What is happening in there? Why aren't I being included in what sounds like a momentous financial decision? With a guy she hardly even knows. How can she be so clueless?

"Okay, I'll definitely think about everything, Dave. And let you know this week."

"I'm glad, Marie. I'm sure you won't regret it," Dave says.

Regret what? More dead air. God, are they kissing again? Or even worse? Mom's been acting like a ridiculous teenager lately. He's probably got his hand under her top. Ewww. That juicy apple pie is staring at me on the counter. I reach for a plate in the cupboard. As I slide it out there's a huge clatter from the stack of plates. I cringe and wait.

"Are you out there, Tara ?" Mom asks.

"Just grabbing a slice of pie. Sorry to disturb you guys," I call back.

"No worries." Dave tells me. "I'm about to head home now anyway. Hope to see you again soon, Tara."

Hope to see you again *never*, dude. Plate in hand with a huge juicy hunk of pie, I skitter down the hall to hide out in my room and try to figure out the meaning of everything I just heard. Clearly my mom is moving forward without me now. Grabbing her chance at a new life, as she describes it. And maybe there's nothing I can do to stop her. But maybe there is, and I know I have to at least take a chance and give it a shot. Before she goes and blows it all yet again.

* * *

My phone doesn't ring Sunday evening. Priya never calls, despite my texts, so I give up. And no call from the ring seeker, either. By Monday morning all my high hopes have plummeted to earth like an out-of-control kite. I desperately need to talk to my mom, but I wake up late and rush right out the door to school, chewing on a granola bar, without even laying eyes on her.

When I reach my locker, breathless and in a rush to beat the bell, Iris is waiting for me. Iris who's playing 'Emily Webb' in *Our Town*. Her eyes are wide, and she looks even more stressed out than I'm feeling. Now what?

"Oh thank goodness. I thought you'd never show up," she say. "I need to talk to you badly about something."

137

"Okay. About what?" I ask as I rummage through my locker.

"About 'Emily Webb'. About playing her role for me."

I spin around and drop a textbook on my foot. "Ouch! What are you talking about?"

As I bend to pick it up, she grabs my arm and yanks, so she's staring me right in the face. She's so good in the role that I actually feel as if I'm looking at Emily.

"Okay, so you won't even believe what happened." She takes a deep breath and stands there blinking madly.

"Well what, for God's sake. Hurry up and spill it, will you!"

"I auditioned for an acting gig on the weekend. For a TV show. And I got the part! I actually got it! I mean, I only have like a couple of lines. But they're shooting it the week of the play, and I have to be there."

"Iris, seriously," I say, feeling a surge of panic. "You want me to take over your role? I haven't even rehearsed it on stage with Silas yet. And the performances start in two weeks! And you're so good!"

"Well, I'm trying to get my ACTRA membership card, see, and I need, like, three acting credits, so…"

"Please stop talking," I tell her, just as the first bell echoes off the walls. "You've been rehearsing for weeks. I haven't! I need to think. And I need to get to class. I'll catch up with you later."

As I dash for my first class, I feel as though my head is floating along behind me like a helium balloon on a string. How can I possibly concentrate on school for the rest of the day? And how will I ever be able to pull this off? How can this even be happening!

It isn't easy to sit there and pretend to be focused. In each class that morning, the teacher's voice is just white noise. In my mind I'm on stage with Silas, playing the part of Emily and trying not to freak out. I run through the scenes in my head over and over again. The one at the soda fountain. All the lines I have to remember that I haven't even gone through once yet with Silas. I can feel my heart beating in my throat. What will happen during the wedding scene that ends with a kiss? How awkward will that be? I'm not nearly ready for this, even if it is just acting. Because after all, it's the great Silas Symonds that I have to fake kiss!

At lunch time I spot Priya in the cafeteria, but she isn't at our usual table. Instead, she's sitting alone with her nose buried in a book, clearly trying to ignore me and everyone else in the room. I sneak up and stand beside her chair. When she realizes someone's there, she looks up slowly and her eyes narrow.

"Did you get my texts?" I ask.

"Got 'em," she says, then looks back at her novel.

Her silence practically steams with simmering anger.

"But...but you never replied." My mouth has gone dry. How stupid is it to feel so uncomfortable around your best friend? "What's wrong, Priya? Be honest with me. Please. I need to know."

She closes her book. When she starts speaking, she never looks up.

"You're not being honest with me, Tara. You hid the fact that Silas was in touch with you." Her voice is stiff and stilted. "I know it's because you think I've got something for him. Which I don't! I just found it totally awkward that I had to sit and watch the two of you stare at each other on Saturday night."

"Huh? What do you mean? All he did was talk about *himself*, Priya."

"Honestly, it felt like I was barging in or something. It was so humiliating." Her face starts to twitch. She can't seriously be about to cry over this.

"But he was just there to rehearse. He's a perfectionist," I try to explain. "I left shortly after you did. I was mad at him for ignoring you. And trust me, I told him off too."

"What?" When she jumps to her feet her chair falls backwards with a huge crash. Everyone turns to look. Her chin is trembling and her eyes all watery. A slow tear slides down her cheek. "How could you do that to me? How can I even be in the same room as him? Now he'll actually think I like him!"

"But you actually *do* like him, don't you?"

"Oh my God, Tara, really. Just shut up." Her wet face is set in a grimace of misery.

She bolts for the cafeteria door and slams out into the hallway. Clearly Priya isn't being honest with me at all, either. Clearly she's crushing hard on Silas. And she's jealous, thinks that I'm getting closer to him. What will happen when she hears the latest news, that I actually have to play the part of Emily Webb? I don't even want to begin to think about that.

But at rehearsal after school that day, there's no hiding the inevitable truth. Ms. Wilding stands right up at centre stage and makes the announcement loud and clear.

"We have some exciting news today," she says, clapping her hands for our attention. She stands there smiling as the cast and stage crew settle into silence. "One of our cast members is going to be in an actual television show. Iris has nabbed a role in a historical detective series on the CBC. Come over here, Iris."

As everyone claps and whoops, Iris sidles up to Ms. Wilding.

"It's just a small role," she says, looking embarrassed. "I'm so pumped, though!"

My eyes search the room for Priya. She's usually right beside me. All the time. And now I can't even see her anywhere.

"Unfortunately, due to the shooting schedule, Iris has to back out of her role as

Emily Webb." Groans all around. "But luckily, she has a capable understudy. Tara Watson. Thanks Tara, for agreeing to step into the part on short notice. I'm sure you'll do an amazing job."

I swallow a huge knot in my throat as everyone around me begins to clap. Then I catch Silas's eye. He's wearing a wide sideways grin, as he shoots me a thumbs up. I try my best to offer him a wobbly smile. I can't figure him out at all. And how am I ever going to pull this off and make it look as if I care, when he's done nothing to help me feel as if I should? When he always seems to make everything about him. I turn away quickly, only to come face to face with Priya. She isn't smiling.

"Looks like that lucky moonstone ring is still working its magic," she says. Then spins around and walks off.

The ring is at home in my drawer. Why hasn't anyone seen those 'found' signs yet and called me up? After all, they were the ones who put the signs up in the first place after losing that creepy ring. The signs that I stupidly tore down, instead of just calling the number. God, what an idiot I've been. I need that jinxed thing gone for good from my life.

Like forever!

* * *

Sophie

Kissing, right there in the shade beside the garage. And they're hugging too. And looking into each other's eyes. The exact same way I've been daydreaming about looking into Silas' eyes since the very first day I ever laid eyes on him.

"What is *happening*?" Lexi shrieks right beside my ear.

"Shut up, they'll hear you," I yelp, then shove her hard so she tumbles sideways off my window seat.

"Hey-*ya*," she whines. "Why did you have to do that? Are you cray or what?"

I slide down beside her and sit there staring straight ahead in a complete daze. Then I slowly turn my head to face my friend.

"OMG I will never un-see that kiss Lex! I can't even believe this. I mean, what clues did I miss? He wants to be an actor and talked about some guy in improv class named Damon, but whatever. And he told me he wanted to be in this play that I've never even heard of. Hedwig and the something-something. Wait."

My phone is in my hand of course so I google it right away. '*Hedwig and the...*' And the words '*Angry Inch*' come up right away. Quickly I scan the synopsis. Then toss my phone into the air as if it burned my hand, catching it before it hits the floor. "Angry Inch!"

I start laughing. Maybe just a little more hysterically than some might consider normal. Lexi sits there watching me and frowning like I might be completely losing it. Finally, I manage to get control of myself, then let out one last hiccup before I offer her a wobbly smile.

"Oka-y-y-y-y, so what was that all about?" Lexi raises one perfectly plucked eyebrow at me. "Now tell me something, were we seeing things or what? I mean what was actually going on down there? Not a waste of two perfectly beautiful males, I hope. That would make me so sad."

I draw in a deep breath. "So, let's just check the clues and see, shall we? Says here that the Hedwig play is a rock musical."

"Okay, that's a good start, right? If he can dance too, then he's a triple threat. Way more opportunities. But why were they even kissing? I don't get it."

"Duh, Lexi. Seems Hedwig is a rock musical comedy about a genderqueer singer. Silas told me he wants to play the lead in it someday."

Lexi's face twists up. "Huh! Okay then. What's an angry inch anyway?"

"Hmm." I scan the synopsis again. Hah! "The angry inch is...well it's...ouch!" When I start laughing again, her eyes grow really wide. "You sure you want to know more?"

"Yikes! Stop," Lexi yelps. "Just stop. I don't need any more details. Oh why, oh why, do all the nicest hottest guys always seem to play for the wrong team? It totally sucks."

What an idiot! She starts scrolling through her phone as if she's already lost interest. Typical Lexi move. Why do I keep on putting up with this?

"Don't be an idiot," I tell her. "That's so not the point. You just always seem to fixate on the hottest guys. And completely write off the ones who don't meet your outrageous standards. But sometimes they aren't exactly the best choices, right? Silas is nice enough, plus gay, but whatevs. He's also kind of egocentric, as far as I could tell. But the truth is, lots of people are."

Maybe even me, come to think of it. And you for sure. Neither of which I say out loud. Wow this is so ridiculous I can't even believe it. How could I have missed all those clues?

"Hmm. I've never been quite clear about the meaning of that word egocentric," Lexi says with a half frown. "Give me an example."

"Well, for one thing, it's always being the centre of your own universe. Always needing to be right. Always expecting everyone to agree with you and do your bidding. Always making everything about you. Remind you of anybody you know, Lex?"

Lexi's too-shiny scarlet-red mouth forms a pout, and she frowns, starts nodding.

"Totally! Lots of people, Soph. And God, I can't stand people like that. I mean, look at me, for instance," she says, staring at her perfect manicure. "I do nice things for people all the time. I even write essays and lab reports and book reports and other stuff for my friends and even my non friends. Who else does that?"

"They pay you for it," I remind her, emphasizing each word. "And that's actually cheating, big time, you know. Jeez. Just saying that makes you egocentric, by the way."

"Hmm. Well I disagree, and you're wrong, because, the truth is, they actually 'reward me' (air quotes) to say thanks for helping out. They don't really have to pay me. But I kind of expect it now, right? And it's just so easy if you know where to source material online. And it's not brain surgery just mixing words and sentences around to make them all sound fresh. So how can it be cheating if you're just fixing things for them to help make it all sound way better, duh. It's sort of like being a tutor, and I'm actually helping people get better marks. So basically, I'm the exact opposite. Non eco-centric!" Smug smirk as she keeps scrolling through her phone and answering text messages like I'm not even sitting right beside her. Her long fake toxic-pink fingernails click madly on her phone screen.

Tutor! That's a *new* one. Lexi sure has worked hard to put a positive spin on what she surely must realize is completely wrong.

Anything to justify her awfully flawed scheme.

"Wow, okay. So it's *ego*, not eco, dude. And that's a perfect example, right there," I tell her. "Egocentric is being so self-centered and self-absorbed that you miss everything else that's going on around you. Only ever focus on yourself. Like you. Right now."

Lexi heaves a huge sigh. "Oh yeah? Huh. Well, whatevs. And it's true, I am kinda bored right now. So, I guess I'll head out since there's nothing else to do here. Total waste of my time. Caitlyn's going to the mall for sushi. Guess I'll head over and meet up with her. Seeya later, babe."

Then she's on her feet and through my bedroom door without even looking back. I sit there stunned for a second then crawl up onto my window seat again for a peek. And lo and behold, she's already out there handing each of the guys one of the cards that she had printed up online. Offering her writing services. Next thing I know she's chatting them up. Through my cracked-open window I can hear her blathering on.

"Wow, you guys are the coolest. I love how you've found each other and have no problem demonstrating affection. You make a great couple." She takes a quick selfie with them, posts it on Insta right away, of course. Smiles at them again. "By the way, this is my card, just in case you ever need any help or guidance with anything like essays and labs and book reports and stuff. I make it my business to help students out. It's my way of giving back."

"Interesting," Zeke says, eyeing her card. "I'll definitely keep that in mind."

"Here to help, anytime," she says, touching his shoulder. "Call or text that number anytime. I can help make your academic problems literally disappear. Presto. Gonzo!" Finger snap.

"Huh, you're almost like a magician, isn't she, Silas?" Zeke says.

"Totally," Silas says. "Takes a special kind of person."

"That's me! Yay, you totally get it! Here, take more cards, tell your friends." She swings her mane of blonde hair as they stand there staring dumbfounded at her. "So. Any questions, boys? Okay, I'm taking that as a no."

Wow. Totally missing the dissing in their words, and their silence. Making herself out to be the hero, as usual. And omitting the complete story, the part about sourcing material online and helping people cheat. If they want more info about what she does to 'give back', it will have to come with the promise of silence. No ratting out allowed, or the wrath of Lexi will fall upon your head. And just before she walks over to her car, she actually gives them each a happy little hug. Egocentric manipulator extraordinaire.

Jeez. It never ends with her!

After Lexi leaves, I try to focus on my World Religion essay for a while. I'm starting to believe that maybe I'm a Buddhist in my soul. I love the whole concept of mantras to keep focused. Of meditation to centre yourself. *Om mane padme hum.* Ancient Buddhist mantra. Compassion is possible when the jewel of the mind rests in the lotus of the heart. The heart/mind connection can liberate you. Help push away negativity. Bring peace to your soul. I love these ideas so much. They feel like the complete opposite of the way Lexi lives her life, and the direction I'd nearly been headed in my own. It's almost comforting to realize that even before I started this essay, I was starting to ask questions about the way my oldest friend operates these days. And how she seems to focus on all the wrong values. I put my thoughts down in point form on the page. But I can't formulate any clear ideas to prove my thesis statement right now.

It's tough to concentrate because of every other crazy thing that's doing laps in my brain circuits. I'm still trying to process what Lexi and I saw out in the driveway. It doesn't matter at all to me that Silas and Zeke are probably a happy new couple. What bugs me is that maybe I was sending Silas all the wrong vibes and he must think I'm a total moron. Or maybe he's just too self-involved and success obsessed to have even noticed. That travesty with the chocolate milk and steamy novel out on the porch was a dead giveaway. It still makes me cringe thinking about it. But it barely even registered with him. I think we need to talk sometime so I can straighten things out with that guy.

Then there's the problem with the ring and Dhanu and our dad. Ugh, the thought that they were probably carrying on right under our noses makes me sick. The fact is, though, they did a pretty good job of hiding their passion. I can't recall ever seeing any hint of what they were up to. They sure did a great job of pulling the wool over our eyes. I'm not sure how I'll ever be able to face Dad again, knowing what he's been up to. It's hard not to despise him right now.

Poor Mom. Somehow or other Jonah and I need to come up with a way to break it to her gently. Yet again today she's off somewhere doing something and making herself scarce. She's always so caught up in her various ways of avoiding what really matters, that she misses the big picture. We need to get this done, and somehow help our mom find her way through processing the big changes that will be coming to her life soon.

I text my brother in his bedroom and offer to take him out for lunch at our favourite local eatery, Sweetest Smoke, so we can figure this out. Because it needs to happen sooner than later before the shit hits the fan. Three seconds later he's in my doorway.

"How did you even guess I've been craving a pulled pork sandwich."

Five minutes later, I've got Dad's key fob in my hand, and we're headed for his Land Rover that's been parked in the garage while he's out of the country.

"I feel no guilt at all for borrowing it without even asking Mom first," I tell Jonah as I'm backing out of the driveway. Silas and Zeke are still shooting hoops. I completely avoid looking their way, still cringing inside out due to my idiotic mistake.

"Hey, check it out," Jonah says. "He's got a friend for you to drool over. Ah, so that's why Lexi showed up out of the blue right after that guy did? How'd that work out for you two?"

"That's Zeke," I tell him, wincing. "They're gay, okay. And I'm so over it now. So please just shut up about it. I beg of you. I mean, I don't know how I could have missed all the obvious clues. But to be honest there really weren't that many. Or maybe I was just ignoring them?"

When I glance sideways at my brother, he has the hugest grin on his face.

"Hah, I wondered when you'd figure that out," he says, and starts laughing hysterically.

"What the hell," I yelp. "You mean you already knew?"

"Yup. Dead giveaway when I saw him making out with some guy behind his house last week. And guess what. It wasn't this Zeke guy, either."

"Come on, seriously? Wow, Silas is a player. Go figure. I should have known by his serious ego problems. Seems like it's all about him, even from the first meeting. You're a jerk for not telling me, you know, and letting me make a complete fool of myself. And now you need to treat me to lunch for being such a loser," I snark at him.

"Oh, and it's so worth it," he says. "Because you should see your face right now."

"Huh," I say, then I elbow his arm really hard, so he'll shut his big stupid mouth.

Sweetest Smoke has the usual Sunday lunch crowd starved for their smoked meat sandwiches and other awesome retro diner fare. I'm drooling just thinking about my favourite chicken sandwich with dipping gravy. But when we reach the entrance, there's a line-up that stretches right out the door.

"We should have known," Jonah groans. "Should have called ahead."

"We can wait, you know. Maybe it won't be that bad. I'll slip inside and ask how long, put our name in for a table. Or better yet, we can maybe do a take-out."

"Perfect. I'll stand in line just in case."

I elbow my way through the dirty looks of waiting diners until I reach the counter. The girl that's standing there is all business.

"How long until a table's available?" I ask, with hope in my voice. Because now that the awesome smoky aroma has hit my nose, my stomach can't wait much longer.

"Oh gosh," she says, checking her computer screen. "Could be at least an hour or even more. You could do take-out but there's a long wait for that too. You could come back in maybe an hour and pick it up though."

"Oh really?" I mutter. "Bad news for my stomach." She offers me a weak smile. "I'll be back in a sec. Just have to find out what my brother wants. I'll be having the chicken sandwich with a side of poutine and cole slaw."

"Good choice," she says. "I'll be right here when you get back, clearly." Eye roll.

I push my way outside through the frowning diners who are likely hangry from waiting so long. But when I reach the end of the line, Jonah isn't there anymore. When I look around I spot him standing near a scrawny tree by the parking lot, and I hurry over.

"Hour's wait, even for take-out. What do you want to order?"

"Nothing," he mumbles. "Lost my appetite." Then he points toward the windows of the diner, where happy eaters are inhaling their meals. "Check it out."

"Check what out?"

"See in that window right there? Recognize anyone?"

I squint in the sunshine. "There's a glare. I can barely even see anyth...oh crap. The headscarf. Let's get out of here before she sees us."

I grab Jonah's sleeve and drag him toward the Land Rover. We leap inside, slam the doors, and just sit there speechless, frozen in time for a moment before I start the engine. My heart is trying to punch its way out of my chest. What is even happening with our family. Beside me, my brother looks nauseous.

"Okay, calm down. So, Mom is sitting in Sweetest Smoke with a strange man." The last thing I need is for my brother's lurking anxiety to completely paralyze him right now. He's way too much like our mom. "Could mean anything, right Jonah, so take it easy, okay. It's all good."

He's breathing in a strange, anguished way. "Oh yeah, sure," he says. "Could mean anything super screwed up. Because guess what. I saw the dude kissing her just now. And trust me, she was totally kissing him back."

I gulp hard as I steer the Land Rover toward home. I'm so perplexed and confused, I feel as if I'm navigating in a blurry fog. Kind of like my whole life right now. So, I try to focus on just getting us home safely.

"Sweet Jesus," I whisper. "How did our family ever get so freaking messed up?"

* * *

Later Sunday afternoon, when Mom comes home looking completely chill, with a wide, soft smile on her face, I don't give her the satisfaction of asking questions. Jonah already decided on the drive home from the diner that we wouldn't even mention it to her.

Now she's just as guilty as our dad. The two of them are clearly cheating on each other, the a-holes. We guilt her into ordering dinner from Sweetest Smoke via Uber Eats, since she hasn't been around much lately. That guilt trip works to perfection, too. So, so sorry kids, she says over and over again as she sets the table for our smoked meat sandwiches and poutine sides. Completely unaware that we know she already ate there today. And was KISSING another man for dessert!

I don't sleep more than about six hours that night and by Monday morning when I stumble out of bed, I figure I'll be stuck with a dazed brain most of the day. It starts out badly too, when I'm charging for the bus stop, trying to catch the second bus, having missed the first. Everything around me is a hurried blur. Until I spot the sign about a RING FOUND.

I stop dead in my tracks. It's on one of the same posts I used to hang the signs Jonah made for me. I rip the sign right off

155

and go hunting for more as the last bus glides
on by.
   Om mane padme hum.

Chapter Seven

Tara

Rehearsal doesn't go well Monday afternoon. I'm sure the entire cast and crew are watching and judging me. I blow almost every line when I have to act opposite Silas alone on stage. He keeps trying to reassure me, but I can tell he's getting frustrated. He starts off smiling, then his face slowly tightens, then he starts sighing and shaking his head. I feel like a complete fool for making him look bad.

Ms. Wilding tells me to relax, that in a few days I'll start feeling the part, like I'm living inside Emily Webb's skin, thinking her thoughts. I highly doubt that, since I can't even figure out how to live inside my own skin. And my thoughts are like a runaway train most of the time. As soon as she says we can go home, I flee the auditorium without looking back and run nearly all the way.

But oh crap! There's a sickeningly familiar old Toyota parked on our street when I get there. The window jerks down. A shaggy head leans out.

"Tara Bear!" My dad. What is he doing here? "Come over here for a sec! I miss you!"

Yeah, right. Whenever my dad shows up, we know that he's desperate for something. He's a lot like a needy little kid who always has to get his own way. If he doesn't, he actually pouts. I shuffle slowly toward his beater car and stop without getting too close.

"What are you doing here, Dad."

"Come over and give me a hug," he says as he climbs from the car and leans against the dented door. His craggy face is forcing a smile, I can tell. "I brought you something."

"Oh, you mean you're dropping off a child support payment?" I don't even try to disguise the sarcasm in my voice. This has been going on way too long.

His face sags as he holds something out. "It's a shoulder bag. A nice leather one."

He probably found it at Goodwill. Or stole it from someone's car. "No thanks. I don't use those. I prefer my backpack. What do you really want, Dad?"

"Suit yourself." He frowns as he pitches the bag through the car window. "So, I heard we struck it rich. How 'bout that, eh? Lucky us!"

My stomach lurches. "Well, guess what. You heard wrong."

"No, I heard *right*. I ran into Lyla. She told me your mom wrote her a cheque. For five grand, apparently. Pretty generous, huh." He smirks. "Still kills when Daddy's right, doesn't it?"

He leans against the car, grinning smugly, still that cocky jackass I remember so well. Always so happy to throw anything awful into our faces just to watch us cringe and die a little inside.

My stomach curdles. Please say Mom didn't do that, actually give her a cheque! And what is the problem with Lyla and her big mouth? Why does my mom always have to choose the wrong people as friends? And why am I always stuck fixing all the ridiculous problems that she's responsible for creating?

"I guess that's her business," I tell him, shoving my trembling hands into my hoodie pocket so he won't notice how nervous I am. "And nobody's rich. Trust me."

He stands there staring at me in the same way as always, with those dark and probing mistrustful eyes. Those eyes have made me nervous for my entire life. And I'm so over it!

"Seventy-five grand is no small potatoes," he says. "Ten grand would really help me out. If you could talk your mother into it. She won't answer the phone. See, I've got this great idea..."

"Forget it. Don't bug her anymore. She has a new boyfriend, and she really likes him. So, you need to stay out of her life. Like for good."

When a storm cloud crosses my dad's face, I take a step back.

"Whaddya mean a new boyfriend?" His voice rumbles. "She's seeing someone? So, who is this asshole? Anyone I know?" His face has turned an unhealthy ruddy shade of purple red.

"Again, it's really none of your business."

And then, before I can blink, his thick hand flashes out and he grabs my arm and squeezes way too hard. "Tell me," he growls, boozy breath in my face. "Right now. Who is this jerk."

I've seen him do the same thing to my mom often enough. He's never tried it on me. Until now. So, I try something I've never ever dared to do in my life so far. Something I've often dreamed of doing too many times, though, when he was hurting Mom. I hoof my dad hard in the shin, and when he yelps and lets go, I take off running. I am so done with the dickhead.

"Stop drinking and driving you idiot," I yell over my shoulder.

"You rotten little bitch," he yells back.

No big deal. I've been called way worse by him. I focus on the sidewalk as I bolt around the corner to get away. He seems worse than ever now, as if all those years of anger and disappointment and failure are bubbling to the surface like poison. And poisoning his whole personality. I hope he won't follow me in his crap can car. Possibly I've humiliated him enough that he's figured it out and will leave me alone. Leave us alone. Forever. We sure don't need him showing up to complicate our lives yet again. And begging for our money. That's apparently disappearing fast, too. Why has she gone and given money to Lyla? Fury shoves me forward. Clearly my mom will never change, never make sound decisions. Never do the smart thing. And I am sick of living this way.

Why does absolutely NOTHING ever work out for me?

My eyes are blurry with tears, and a furious desperation is welling up inside my chest. I'm so angry I want to scream at the sky, at the whole world. Until I run smack into the back of something and land hard on my butt on the sidewalk. When I look up, dazed, I realize that the 'something' is actually someone. A girl, maybe about my age. Dressed in a school uniform.

"Oh my God, I'm so sorry. I didn't mean to crash into you. I was kind of in a hurry and I wasn't paying attention." I start dragging myself to my feet.

The girl looks as stunned as I'm feeling. Then her face breaks into a wide smile.

"Are you okay," she asks, reaching her hand out to help me to my feet. Her blondish shiny hair falls like a veil around her face. And in that instant I can guess exactly who she is. The girl who lost her moonstone ring.

"It's you," I whisper, gazing into her wide grey eyes. "Isn't it?"

She looks at me, head tilted. "What do you mean," she says. "And are you alright? I'm sorry I got in your way. You really must be in a huge hurry. And you look freaked out, too."

"Just trying to get away from my dad," I tell her, brushing off the seat of my jeans.

And right that moment, his crappy car creeps around the corner. "Tara Bear," he calls out the window. "I'm so sorry. I didn't mean it. Forgive me please. Let's just talk, okay?"

"Go away, please Dad," I half sob, half yell. "Just leave Mom and me alone!"

His face turns all sad, like I've hurt his feelings, not that he's ever had any. Not that he's ever cared about me unless it's to try and get something out of me. "Come on, honey. You know you want to help your good old dad out. Think of all the great times we've shared. Remember when we always used to go out for ice cream together..."

"That you stole from the freezer of the convenience store. Oh, gee yeah, that was so much fun, Dad. Getting chased down the street by the clerk. And how about that time you took me to buy a book—at the *library*. You actually stole it from the shelf! Real good times!"

"You're such a thankless little bitch, you know. Exactly like your mom," he snarls. His window zooms up and he takes off with a screech of tires and a puff of stinky smoke.

The girl stands there looking utterly horrified, and I don't blame her. How embarrassing for her to witness this awful private incident. She must think my family is completely trashy.

"Oh my God, I'm so sorry you had to see that," I murmur swallowing the lump in my throat.

Then the look on her face morphs into thoughtful and distant. "Wow, brutal. Clearly he's done something major to piss you off, right?"

"He always does," I tell her, scrubbing at my wet eyes. "It's never good when he shows up." Why do I feel so comfortable talking to this girl that I've never met in my life. "Whenever he drops by everything seems to fall apart. It's so frustrating. I mean, I wish I could love him, but he always finds a way to ruin everything," I over-explain with a watery sniffle. "Oh jeez, I'm sorry. I'm blathering. It's just that he showed up out of nowhere and took me by surprise."

She half smiles and shakes her head. Wow, to have silky golden hair like hers. In my dreams. "No worries. I know the feeling well. Trust me. You would not even believe what my dad just did. He completely screwed over our whole family." She squints as her face turns steely. "I'm trying to figure out if I hate him, or I just despise him, or if they're maybe the same thing."

"Oh crap. That sucks." I sniffle again, maybe a bit too loud. "You know, it's just that

I feel like I've hit a wall with this guy." I wipe my eyes on my sleeve.

"Sometimes that happens," she murmurs with a sad voice, and her fury seems to seep out of her almost as if she's given up. "Sometimes it just gets to a point where you have to let it go and move on, I guess, or it just eats away at you. I'm trying hard myself. And it sucks. It really does. Look, I'm sorry I can't talk to you longer. But I'm in a bit of a hurry to get home."

"Oh, that's okay," I tell her. "Honestly, you came along at just the right moment. Sorry for dumping on you like that."

"Again, no worries," she says, then reaches out and squeezes my hand. "Gotta run!"

"Wait one second," I say, touching her arm. "Did you...by any chance...lose something sparkly around here recently? Maybe?"

Her face sags. Her eyes widen. "No, no, no! I have to go now," she says. Then she spins around and darts off like a scared squirrel.

"At least give me your phone number," I call behind her. "So, we can talk again. What's your name anyway?"

She doesn't look back. And I can't even figure out why I said that. Talk again? What's your name? I'm such a dork! She must think I'm a desperate friendless stalker. But maybe I felt a connection because her whole face seemed to soften when she heard my problem, as if she totally understood my dilemma. Clearly she's a sister in sorrow with her own set of ugly problems that she's trying to wrap her head around. But why did she react that way when I mentioned losing something? It just has to be her ring.

That's when it hits me. All the RING FOUND signs are gone. On every pole I check. What is even happening with that jinxed ring?

By the time I've backtracked to my house, there's no sign of Dad's car on the street. When Mom doesn't answer my knock, I unlock the door and drop my backpack in the hallway. Then I head straight for the battered desk in the living room where I know Mom keeps all her banking stuff. I have mixed feelings about snooping. On the one hand, I know it's none of my business. But on the other, I need proof of what she plans on doing with the money she won, so I can confront her about the heap of bad choices she's been making.

And when I dig out her cheque book, it's just as I suspected. A big fat cheque for big mouth Lyla, five thousand dollars. A cheque for David Petrie for twenty-five thousand! Another one for five thousand, made out to a name I don't even recognize. So much gone already, in less than a week. I need to stop her before we're broke all over again.

Just as I start scrounging around in the fridge for some dinner and wondering where Mom is, the 'land line' rings. Usually most calls are from telemarketers, and sometimes I answer, just to play head games with them. But when I check the call display, it's Silas. What? Why is he even calling me? I almost don't want to pick up, but what if it's important. Maybe he's calling to tell me that Iris realized just how unprepared I am for this role and decided she won't let her whole cast down after all. Huh, fat chance that ever happening. Finally, I snatch up the phone and practically bellow hello.

"Wow, that was loud! How's it going, Tara?" he says. "You disappeared really fast today. And I need to talk to you about the George and Emily scenes. Because..."

"Look, Silas, I know that I stink at playing Emily, so you don't have to rub it in. I was just totally freaked out on stage today. It felt like everyone was comparing me to Iris..."

"Well, they aren't," he says. "You're just imagining it. You need to try and relax, okay?"

I let out a noisy sigh. "I don't know if I can do this, Silas," I confess. "I'm not experienced enough. I'll ruin it for the whole cast."

And I'm just not feeling it with *you*, I can't help but think. Why exactly, I'm not sure. Maybe it's because while we're rehearsing, all I can think about is Priya out there hating me. And it's been crushing my soul.

"Look, we have to find a way to make it work. You can do this, Tara. How about we get together later tonight and go over our most crucial scenes."

Hmm. He sounds sincere enough. And really nice, now that it isn't all about him. It sounds as if he honestly wants to help me.

"I guess we should," I tell him. "So where do you want to meet up?"

"You can come to my place if you want," he suggests. "We can rehearse in the rec room. It's a pretty good size for blocking."

Way better than at my place. I always avoid bringing anyone home because of our crappy circumstances. And our basement is an unfinished dump stacked with boxes of junk we've never unpacked since moving there after we ditched my dad. So, I make a snap decision.

"Okay. What time?" And that's when I know that I'm completely committed.

"Six thirty is good," he says. "If you haven't eaten yet, we can order pizza."

"Sounds great. I'm starved. Wait...where do you live?"

"Oh, that might help," he says with a low chuckle. The one that makes all the girls crazy. I give him my new cell phone number and he texts me his address right after he hangs up.

Now I'm feeling even more nervous. I don't want to let him down and look like a doofus. I want him to trust that I can pull this off. And I need to stop doubting myself, to be better than ready for this, so I head for my room to go over that script a few times before even leaving for his place. Silas is so right. We need to make this work so we won't both look like fools on stage. It's time for me to stop worrying about who's thinking what, and to do the right thing.

Priya can let her imagination run as wild as she wants. She can blame me, or forgive me, or whatever. But I know I can't allow myself to take any more of the blame if I'm going to make this work. I need to let it go and move on, something a complete stranger that I randomly met, suggested to me today. Someone who is probably the true owner of the moonstone ring, judging by the way she reacted. But why did she deny it? What is with this peculiar ring and the reactions it seems to trigger in everyone who touches it?

That's when I decide that tomorrow after school, right around the same time that I ran into her today, I plan on staking out that spot and giving the ring back to its rightful owner once and for all.

I won't take no for an answer either.

* * *

Sophie

After running into that girl, the one who clearly found the ring, I run all the way home from the bus stop. She looks really familiar too. I've seen her before. I'm almost positive. And it's utterly insane, the way we just met. It's uncanny really, how so many random things have happened since that creepy moonstone ring landed in, and then disappeared, from our lives. And the reason I bolted, is that I'm not positive I actually want to see the jinxed thing ever again. Which is why those signs I found on the posts this morning are in my backpack now. I wonder if she noticed them missing.

Mom's BMW is in the driveway for a change. Something twists in my gut at the thought of her sitting in Sweetest Smoke with some complete stranger. Head to head, making out, ugh, and totally oblivious to the fact that her two kids are standing outside watching them. It's a crushing new development in our totally screwy family life.

I shove my way through the front door, yell hello to nobody, then tear straight up the stairs to my bedroom. Behind my closed door, I pull out the signs, slide them into my shredder, then drop the paper shreds into my recycle bucket. I feel so stupid for doing this, because I really should have done the right thing and confessed to losing the ring to that girl who crashed into me today. And just sucked it up and handed over the reward money, which I haven't even figured out yet. And then handed the ring back to Mom. Just to see the look on her face.

Has she moved on from her sadness at missing Dhanu since she doesn't have the ring to remind her anymore? She has a ton of explaining to do. But then again, I guess that won't happen until Jonah and I start demanding some explanations ourselves. Which needs to happen soon. I text my brother asking where he is, and seconds later he blasts into my room slamming the door behind him.

"Yikes! You scared the crap out of me, Jonah! Why didn't you answer me when I yelled hello a couple of minutes ago?" I ask him.

"Ear buds, duh." He rolls his eyes.

"So, what's the next move?" I ask as he sits cross-legged on my floor.

"You tell me," he says. "I can't stop thinking about it, and it's starting to totally stress me out. I'm getting this sort of numb feeling in my cheeks sometimes. And I feel like I'm going into a sort of daze that I can't snap out of."

I feel a sudden tightness in my own chest. This can't be a good sign, these symptoms that Jonah is experiencing. I hate the thought of him starting to crack over this. So, I sit facing him.

"You have to try and relax," I tell him in a gentle tone. He actually looks scared now.

"I googled the symptoms," he says, wide-eyed. "Major signs of anxiety. Which is sort of good and bad. I was scared something way worse was wrong with me."

"Honestly, that's bad enough. Think back to when Mom lost it a few years ago. You need to work on it right away. To stay ahead of your symptoms," I tell him. Maybe he needs meds too?

"I know, I'm working on it. I even googled help for anxiety. Found out it's genetic."

"Of course it is. Well, I guess online research is a good start." I sit there and stare into his troubled green eyes that look hauntingly like our mom's have in the past. A deep and disturbing worry gazes back at me. "Everything will be fine. Try and take some deep breaths when you're anxious."

"What good will that do?" he asks in a raspy voice. His chin trembles a little. "It sure won't make all the fucked-upness in our family go away, will it? Why can't we just be like a normal family?"

I laugh a little at that one. "Because there is no normal family. So, I ran into this girl today on the sidewalk. Well, she ran into me. And guess what? She was running away from her jerk of a dad who was stalking her in his car. She poured out all her crap to me, a random stranger that she just met. No, there is no normal family, Jonah, I swear."

"Really? She told you all that?" He sniffs and gulps hard. Takes a deep breath.

"She told me that everything falls apart when her dad shows up. Her family is totally effed up too, obviously. We are not alone. And guess what. I think she might be the person who found the ring. She asked me if I lost anything 'sparkly' lately." I don't even mention the signs I tore up.

"Wow, really? So, are you getting it back for Mom? Maybe if she has it again, she'll become obsessed with the ring again. And she'll forget about that dude in the diner."

"Okay, so that's some magical thinking right there. Never happening Jonah. In fact, I think she isn't mentioning the ring because she's over it now. She's moved on. Do we really even want that ring back in the house now that we know what's going on with Dad and Dhanu?" Just the thought of it makes me shiver.

"Yeah, you have a point," he tells me as he gives his head a quick shake. "Go away, numbness," he says, slapping his cheeks.

Oh God, now THIS new worry is stressing me out, along with everything else.

"*Om mane padme hum,*" I murmur in a droning singsong voice, making finger circles. "*Om mane padme hum.*"

"Huh? What the hell does that even mean?"

I grin at Jonah, who looks totally perplexed, then start explaining my newfound interest in an ancient Buddhist mantra. Maybe World Religion isn't so boring after all.

"Om money paddy hum?" he says, curling his finger and thumb, and I laugh.

"Pronounce it like this. I listened to it online. Ohm manay padmay hoom."

He says it with me as we sit on the floor staring at each other. "I feel stupid," he says.

"Well, you should be used to that feeling by now, right?" We both laugh.

"So, what's the next move anyway? Do we confront her?"

"Yes. Yes, we definitely do," I tell him. "Maybe at dinner tonight. After she pours a glass of wine. Hopefully she gets dinner on the table before nine o'clock for a change. Okay, I need to get to work on my frigging essay."

"Sounds like Mom's home. I can hear some pots rattling around down there," Jonah says as he's leaving my room. "Maybe that's a good sign."

"Fingers crossed. Close my door please."

I hunker down over my laptop, trying to get words on the page, any words. I'm making some headway on this thing, and getting kind of wrapped up in the whole concept of what it means to be a Buddhist too. I love being in the zone, when you lose all concept of time. It means you're really making progress. And no bouncing yet, thank Buddha.

But right around six-thirty I hear some commotion out in Silas's driveway. Knocks on his door and then voices. And since it's become somewhat of a nasty habit of mine lately, I creep over to my window seat to spy on him again. Wonder if Zeke is back. I don't even know what's going on in that house. I've never laid eyes on his parents because they always pull their two Audi's into the double garage. And I guess since I started crushing on Silas when I first saw him out in the driveway after spring finally showed up late, I've been fixated a little too much. Now I can never resist, even though I know he has a boyfriend or maybe a couple of them.

Silas is greeting someone at the door, and this time it isn't a guy. But yikes! Is that who I think it is? She's wearing the exact same clothes. From her profile it looks like the exact same face too. What in the name of Buddha is she doing at his place? Next thing I know, she's gone inside, and he's shut the door. Now all that's left is me and my twisted imagination taking me places that I don't even want to go. Wow, is he bisexual or fluid or what? Okay don't jump to dumb conclusions. Maybe she's there to study with him or run lines or something. Of course! That's gotta be it. It comes as sweet relief when Mom yells up the stairs for us to come down for dinner a while later.

Awesome smells are drifting up the stairway as Jonah and I race each other to the bottom. My stomach is grumbling. I need sustenance. And ugh, we need to talk to her like we planned earlier. As soon as I sit down,

Jonah tips his head in the direction of the gigantic glass of red wine in Mom's hand as she stands stirring something fragrant on the stove. She takes a big gulp, then turns around and winks at us. Now's our chance, before she starts serving.

But before I can even open my mouth, I can tell by her face that I shouldn't bother.

"I'm glad you're both here, kids," she says, waltzing over to the table in her usual dramatic way. All caftan and scarves and beaded semi-precious gemstone bracelets. "I've made a lovely rich beef bourguignon. But before we eat, there's something I really need to talk to you about." She pulls out a chair and sits down slowly.

"Oh, um, okay," I tell her. What's this now? Under the table, Jonah nudges my foot.

"Like what," he says, barely even able to hide his seething anger. Maybe the anger is a good thing. Maybe it will help to distract him from his lurking anxiety.

Mom takes another gulp of wine and sets down her glass. She places her hands palms up on the table. "Put your hands in mine, okay."

"Wh-h-h-h-y-y-y-y?" Jonah drags the word out, frowning as I give Mom my hand.

"So, I can feel your vibes," she says. With an eyeroll, Jonah gives over his hand. "There we go, kids. Now I'll be able to actually feel your reactions when I try and explain a few things. Ah, I can see that you're already tense, Jonah."

"Wow, you must be a mind reader or a medium or something. Can you talk to the dead, too? Madame Frances. Purveyor of all things mystical." Jonah half smirks after his good line.

Mom just sighs and looks over at me with the same green eyes as my brother.

"If you have something sarcastic to say to me now, Sophie, just let it out. We need to clear the air before I can even start trying to tell this tale."

"I'm all good, so carry on," I tell her, holding back a sigh.

"Yes, your hand is far more relaxed than Jonah's. Hmm. Maybe I need to clear the air in this room before we even begin."

She lets go of our hands then goes over to the little nook where she keeps her special tools. Takes out her abalone shell and smudge stick, and carefully lights it with a wooden match, blows out the flame, then starts to tiptoe as she holds the smoldering stick aloft. This is nothing new to us. We just tolerate it.

"So, the smoke will help to carry away all the negativity," she tells us, practically floating around the main floor and circling back to the kitchen. "Let your gloomy thoughts float away with the smoke. Welcome back positivity into your hearts and souls. Cleanse your mind. Let go of doubt and despair and let peace wash over your beings."

"Oh, give me a break Mother. I should have found someplace else to go tonight," Jonah groans.

Mom swirls smoke past us. "That's it! Let go of all your frustration and hostility, Jonah."

"Yes Mom, we are aware of what we should be doing. *Om mane padme hum. Om mane padme hum*," I repeat, making finger circles, and then Jonah joins me in the chant. "*Om mane padme hum.*" Then our mom does too, in a voice that's absolutely humming with elation.

"*Om mane padme hummmm.*" She floats over to the table, wide-eyed and smiling, as she waves the smoldering stick and wafts smoke. "What's this? Do you mean to say that you're both on the path to enlightenment and you didn't even bother to tell me? This is the best news ever!"

"I just learned about it, Mom," I start explaining. "Because of an essay I'm working on for World Religion. And I told Jonah about it. And I think I could really embrace Buddhism, you know, since I already feel as if..."

"Alright already. Can we just get on with this, before I starve to death," Jonah growls. "Can you both just drop the mystical witchery crap. And please tell us what the hell is going on now, Mom, before my head explodes or something?"

I can tell by his tight jawline that he's scared of what he might be about to hear. As am I.

"Oh, I'm so sorry, sweetie," Mom says, as Jonah cringes. "You know, you're so much like me, which is lovely because it makes you more sensitive than most people. But you don't handle the unknown very well. And I've noticed some major mood swings that can't really be blamed on puberty. That's okay, though. I have a feeling you might have cyclothymia, like I do. And once we get to the bottom of it, and get some therapy for you, maybe some ADs...."

"Don't try and tell me what's wrong with me, Mom. You have no idea what's going on inside my head. And did you ever think that maybe you and Dad are the reasons for my mood swings? God, you both make me so sick." His stilted voice echoes the depth of his anguish.

As I sit there gaping at our mother, Jonah stands up, grimaces, and walks out of the room. She has no clue how hard all this angst-ridden crap is affecting him. Mom sets the smudge stick into the abalone shell to burn out.

"Jonah, come back," she calls after him, her face ridden with self-doubt now. "I didn't mean to be so blunt. I was only trying to help. We can eat now, honey!"

"Just leave him," I tell her. "I'm pretty sure he lost his appetite. But he'll find it again."

She takes my hands again, gazes into my face, long and lingering and loving.

"You are such a good sister, Sophie. So, there's something you should know about the ring," she says. "And exactly how it came into my possession. And why."

Here we go, I can't help but think. The truth will set you free.

"Okay, go for it, Mom. At this point I'm ready for anything and nothing will surprise me anymore."

"I actually, um..." she gulps and blinks. "Well, the fact is, the moonstone ring from Dhanu? She didn't *technically* give it to me. After I figured out that she was having an affair with your dad, I snatched it from her room. And she didn't even notice! That's why I need to get it back. So, I can return it to her and move on. Wow, it sure feels good to get that off my chest."

Huh? That is probably the last thing I ever expected to hear coming from her mouth.

"Are you freaking joking, Mom," I can't help but say to her. "You already knew about those two! And you actually STOLE the ring?"

"Look Sophie, your dad and I were done ages ago. I had guessed a couple of months back about those two carrying on behind our backs. I've been playing dumb and watching carefully. Dhanu thought she was messing with me. But I've been messing with both of them. All along. They call it woman's intuition for a reason, you know. I've been ready for this for a very long time."

I'm pretty much speechless, and I might feel a bit dizzy, from shock or elation or relief.

"Mom. This is the best news I've heard in ages. No wonder you've been acting so bizarre lately with all this stuff going on. You're amazing for handling everything so well."

"And well medicated, too," she adds with a wry chuckle. "But that ring thing is eating at me from the inside out. After Dhanu left, she emailed me, because she realized she was missing her ring. And I let on that I had no clue where it was. Now I've come to realize that I did a very stupid thing. And I need to find a way to fix it. So I can move on with the next phase of my life. I need to, you know, shake off the bad karma from what I did."

I get out of my chair to sidle up behind her and hug her shoulders, squeeze so hard that she gasps and laughs, then lays her head against my hands. Wow, I've been totally misjudging my mom all along. She is absolutely not who I thought she was. She's been getting herself a life, and I didn't even notice, since I'm always so caught up in my own drama. Yup, now's the perfect time to tell my own story. Might as well just clear the air right now.

"So anyway, there's something else you need to know about that damn ring. Because you actually didn't lose, or misplace it, after all."

"Oh really?" Mom says through narrowed yet curious eyes. "Do tell."

Chapter Eight

Tara

I keep dwelling on the mess I'm in the entire time I pedal my bike over to Silas's place. The moonstone ring has got to belong to that girl. Her school blazer colour was the same as that distant blur I spotted when I found it just last Friday. But who the heck is she, and why haven't I noticed her around here before? She obviously gets on and off the bus, comes through this neighbourhood every day. I guess when you aren't really looking, when you're always wrapped up in your own dopey problems, you don't bother to notice the everyday things going on in your life, and you miss so much. I need to pay more attention to every single thing from now on.

And why did her face change so much when I mentioned the ring? Why did she seem so freaked out and dash off? I need to know. I wish she'd said her name. I wish she'd stuck around longer. I wish I could have put that ring into her hand. Enough with the wishes. I just need to be rid of that jinxed ring once and for all, so I can tell Priya I finally did the right thing and we can hopefully pick up where we left off, my best friend and me.

Maybe then my luck, or my fortunes, or my karma or my whatever will finally change.

Silas's house is in a really nice neighbourhood, a fairly recent new development right in our area, built on the site of a long-gone plaza. Double car garages, spacious lots, well-tended gardens with bright swaths of spring flowers. I park my bike around the side of the garage and knock on the side door. Softly at first, and then harder as my courage starts to grow. I really need to own this moment. But why is he taking so long? Did I get the right night? Just as I'm feeling more than freaked out, and almost ready to bolt, Silas opens the door, smiling in his sweet way.

"Sorry, I just got out of the shower," he says.

He looks fresh scrubbed, his dark hair still damp, his face flushed. He's dressed in faded jeans and a white t-shirt with a plaid shirt overtop. Oh, and that sideways smile of his. It's getting easier to understand why so many of the girls have developed mad crushes on this guy ever since he showed up at our school right after the Christmas break. I guess I'm glad I can get to know him better by rehearsing together. Maybe now I won't be so intimidated on stage.

"Hey Silas, or should I say George," I tell him, grinning.

"Hey, how are you, Emily," he says. Then he actually hugs me, as if I really am his girlfriend Emily. "Come on in."

He leads me into a wide hallway. I stop for a second and just stare at everything. It's the sort of house my mom has always dreamed of owning. Big rooms, gleaming furniture, hardwood flooring, plush area rugs, nothing worn or broken, the best of everything. Some alt rock music is playing—from speakers in the ceiling! Otherwise, the house seems empty.

"Where's your fam?" I ask, still looking around.

He kind of freezes and gets a funny look on his face.

"Oh, they went out to grab groceries to cook some spicy Indian curry dinner, which I don't really like. Hence the pizza. They'll be back anytime now."

"So, where's that pizza you promised anyway? I even brought cash to help pay for it."

"On the way. Should be here soon. Hope you're okay with pepperoni, mushroom and onion. If you aren't too weak from hunger, maybe we can rehearse until it shows up."

That makes me grin. One-track mind, this guy. I follow him down a curving staircase to the basement. Shiny ceramic tiles, a gym room, a gigantic TV set up in front of leather lounge chairs. One wide room is practically empty, except for a pool table on one end, and a bar with high stools on the other.

"The party room," he explains. "And also a good space to rehearse."

Then he launches right into his first lines as 'George' speaking to 'Emily'. And now, with just the two of us, with nobody watching, maybe I can get it right.

Just as Ms. Wilding predicted, after a few focused moments, I almost feel as if I'm becoming Emily Webb as I feed her lines back to Silas. I hardly even miss a cue, and I can see his face morphing as he grows more comfortable playing opposite me. As he lets himself become George Gibbs. And we nail their passionate discussion in Act Two about being 'naturally good', and their 'important talk' during the soda fountain scene.

In the big scene just before the wedding when they promise to love and care for one another and then fall into each other's arms, Silas hugs me like he means it. And I freeze up in his arms because I know what's coming next. We follow the stage directions as best we can without the other actors present.

'The ring.

The kiss.

The stage is suddenly arrested into silent tableau.'

And that's when he does it. What I've been either anticipating or dreading all this time. He cups my chin in his hands, and his dark chocolate eyes are gazing right into mine, and he fake kisses me. Just a gentle lingering peck as the scene freezes.

And yikes! His lips pressed against mine are so soft! I feel a hot blush burning on my face. My first kiss ever and it's only pretend. Do I wish it was real? Do I? He lets me go, backs away and smiles.

"And then we *'run up the aisle joyously'*. Okay, so that wasn't so bad, was it?" he says. "I could tell you were nervous. But I wanted to prove to you that this is not only about acting, but about how we react to one another. About really getting into the part, owning your character. I wanted to break the ice with you once and for all. You did a great job, Tara. You will shine on that stage, just like the moon in the play."

"*The moonlight's so wonderful,*" I say, quoting one of my lines, which makes him grin. "*Wow*, thanks, Silas. High praise. And yeah, I kind of think it worked," I tell him as my face starts cooling off. Then I fan myself, and instantly feel foolish for doing it, in case he thinks it means something else. Because right now, I feel, well, absolutely *nothing*. Which seems kind of weird, when I expected the complete opposite, as if I should be half swooning and lovestruck. "Sure hope I don't blush so hard during the play. But at least I won't need make-up if that happens!"

We both crack up and that helps to break all the awkward tension even more. And then the doorbell rings and the pizza shows up and we start chowing down.

And then, a few minutes later, two women come bustling in through the garage doorway with armloads of groceries. Hmm. What's going on here, I wonder? They seem super nice, all smiley and welcoming as they nod their heads hello at me.

"So, this is my Aunt Hazel and her wife, Maggie," Silas says. "I'm living with them."

"Oh, okay." Every word that I need to say, or think I should, is stuck inside my mouth. I don't even know how to respond. "Hello. I'm um...I'm...uh..."

"This is Tara, who seems to have forgotten her name," Silas tells them with a chuckle. "Remember I mentioned her before."

"Right, I remember," Hazel says. "Understudy for Emily Webb."

"That's a great role," Maggie says. "Maybe you'll get lucky and have to fill in."

"Funny you should mention that," Silas says, then starts explaining how lucky I am.

Why does Silas live with his aunt and her wife? Instead of with his folks? Guess it would be nosey to ask though. They both seem so sweet and understanding and real. Even though they aren't his actual parents. It would be awesome if I had a family half as cool as this one. Hah. Oh how I wish, but right now it's more nightmare than it is daydream. And my heart secretly breaks, the way it so often does when I start making wishes that will never come true.

Then Silas and I go over the parts a few more times, performing in front of his two aunts because they beg us to watch. And he helps to guide me through that final scene, Emily's soliloquy, the scene that scares me the most. The one with the infamous, indelible line: '*Do any human beings ever realize life while they live it—every every minute?*' He actually shows me how to say it with passion. There's no doubt about it. Silas is actually helping me to become a better actor. When his aunts clap and tell us how impressed they are, I relax even more. Maybe I really can pull this thing off after all. Maybe this is finally my moment to shine, just like Silas said.

When we say bye at the door a while later, I start feeling super charged all over again. That moonstone ring in my pocket is still working its magic, it seems. I brought it along just for good luck, and somehow it still makes me feel as if I can handle any situation. Or maybe it's just magical thinking. Whatever it is, I like this feeling, as if my bike is flying along, a metre above the actual roadway. As if I'm suddenly living a dream moment that I wish would never end.

Until I spot the white cube van in our driveway when I reach our street. And I almost feel my high spirits hitting the ground with a dull hard thud. Because Dave's car is parked on the road. There's some commotion at the front door. A couple of moving guys hauling boxes. But I can't tell if they're going in or coming out.

"Now what, Mom," I murmur as I wheel into the driveway.

Mom steps out onto the cramped front porch and smiles in an almost scary way. With so much newfound confidence it almost makes me want to shudder.

"Honey, I've been waiting for you! You never answered your cell phone."

My cell phone is in my backpack. I haven't even glanced at it all evening.

"I had other stuff on my mind, Mom. And I was kind of busy. So, what's going on now, anyway?" I dread her answer because I'm pretty sure I already know it.

"Guess what? We're moving," she says with another wide and almost demented smile. And I drop my bike, and it feels as if all the blood in my body has turned ice cold.

"What! Like *tonight*?" Now I'm almost positive that my mom is totally losing it. And that dream moment just burst like the flimsy soap bubble it pretty much was.

"This weekend. First load is going right now. We have this truck at our disposal for a few evenings, and Dave brought a couple of friends over."

"Mom, you're freaking me out! Why haven't I heard about this? What. Is. Happening?"

I follow her inside. I've only been gone for under three hours, and the townhouse is in complete disarray. Furniture in the middle of the room, boxes empty and half packed scattered everywhere. Pots and pans strewn throughout the kitchen, half empty drawers and cupboards. I plop down in an armchair and stare at my mom. She won't meet my gaze though.

"Explain please. What are you even doing, Mom. This looks like a picture of crazy."

My mom finally sits down on a stool and stares back at me, blinking like she's on the verge of tears. "I realize that this is kind of unexpected, Tara, but it came up so suddenly. We have a very small window of opportunity to move into a rental house not far from here. But it has to happen immediately. Otherwise, we lose out."

"It's a good decision, trust me," Dave says, slipping an arm around my mom. "We're just moving a few things tonight, like some armchairs, and boxes from the basement. But as you can see, the packing process is well underway. I picked up a pile of boxes from the liquor store."

I just stare at the two idiots and shake my head in disbelief. I want to bolt from the utter insanity, but I have nowhere to go. Clearly Priya's place is out of the question right now. No, I'm stuck here with a crazy lady and her geeky new boyfriend that she barely even knows, and they both look like wild-eyed weirdos.

"Gee, thanks Mom. I absolutely love how I get included in all these random deranged decisions you've been making lately."

"Come on, Tara, please don't be mad. You'll love this place, I promise. It's on a nice residential street in our same neighbourhood. It's a wee two-bedroom, and even has a finished rec room. You can have friends over, like you've always wanted. It's the closest to normal that we've ever been, I'm telling you. Please trust me right now." Her eyes are pleading with me to believe in her for a change, but that isn't so easy right now.

True enough, I've always wanted to ditch this place. How great would it be with no more leaky faucets and broken appliances. No more soggy drywall and plugged toilets. It almost sounds too good to be true, which is why it's just so hard to believe. Plus, there are still a couple of other burning issues.

"We had a visitor today," I say, and Mom's happy face turns upside down. "Dad was parked on the street when I got home after rehearsal. He heard about the lottery money. From Lyla. He told me you wrote her a cheque for five grand. And he'd like ten grand. Why would your so-called friend blab to Dad? And why did you give her money?"

Mom's nostrils flare. Dave squeezes her shoulder.

"It's complicated," she says. "And don't worry. He's not touching a cent of our money."

"I'm all ears," I tell her.

She sucks in a deep breath. "Last time I kicked your dad out, I had to borrow that money from Lyla. And another five thousand from an old friend who lives out of town. We were in dire straits, seriously, Tara. You had to know this. Rent, food, clothes, you name it. Your dad cleaned out the last of our piddly savings. We had nothing." Her face goes all wobbly for a second.

"What a complete creep," I growl. "You'll be happy to know that after he grabbed my arm and squeezed way too hard, I booted him in the shin. I've wanted to do that for ages. He was a complete jerk today, as usual." My heart beats faster just thinking about it and I swipe away at sudden tears before anyone notices.

"Wow!" Mom's eyes crinkle at the edges and she smirks. "Best news I've heard about him in ages," she says. "And he's had it coming for a long time."

"But why did Lyla have to go and tell him that? What's her problem?"

Mom shrugs. "Lyla's not even sure about that herself. She ran into him at a bar on the weekend. And he started ragging on her for being friends with me and saying all kinds of rotten things about me. So, she just blurted it out, sort of to stick up for me, I guess."

"Oh." I sigh. "Yeah, I don't blame her. That's what real friends do." I miss you, Priya!

"Isn't there something else you wanted to tell Tara?" Dave says.

Alarm bells jangle in my brain. "*What*?" Please don't tell me you're getting married!

"I've invested a lump sum. In an education fund. So, you can go to college. It was Dave's idea. Your dad can't touch it. The rest will be safe now too. A nice nest egg in my own account. And I'm hoping to run a little esthetics place out of a room in the basement of our new house. Lyla will help me. Manis, pedis, waxing, facials etcetera. We're calling it Marla Spa."

"For real?" I ask. And they both nod. "That's...absolutely...awesome. Thanks, Mom. I don't even know what to say." I sit there nodding slowly, feeling dumbfounded. And regretting all the nasty things I've been saying to my mom lately. Maybe this time she really is getting her act together. "Guess I'd better start packing soon, huh?" I say, heading for my bedroom.

"Yup, I'm going to need plenty of help this week. Because we're out of here for good on Saturday," Mom tells me. "Thank God."

In my room, I flop down on my bed and pull that freakish ring out of my pocket. No doubt about it. My life is sliding out of control. Mom has changed. She's making decisions without me. No stopping her stubborn streak to do everything her way. But maybe that isn't such a bad thing after all. This sudden move to a new place has come at the worst possible time though. How will I possibly fit everything in this week, packing, school work, rehearsals?

I lie on my bed, staring at the ring and trying to figure things out. Maybe I never had control over anything to begin with. Maybe I need to accept the fact that, like what my mom said the other day, everything happens for a reason. And maybe the two of us, Mom and me, really are on the cusp of change this time. Maybe she just needed the right motivation to help her move forward with her life. And maybe she's got more smarts and courage than I give her credit for. Because I was blaming her for everything that's gone wrong in our lives, when it's not her fault. Being married to a guy like my jerk dad has got to leave permanent scars on your soul.

And the truth is, I have no control over the way Priya is feeling. She's doing it to herself. When she sees Silas and me on stage at rehearsal tomorrow rocking the George and Emily parts, she's bound to feel even worse. But what's more important to me in the greater scheme of things? Feeling good on stage by taking some sort of big ego trip to prove something to myself, even if my best friend can't handle it and it's breaking her heart? Or by trying to find a way to make it up to her so she knows how incredibly important she is to me?

There's really only one good way to do that, as far as I'm concerned. So, I make up my mind then and there. Since I still have a shred of control over my own life, tomorrow I will try my best to fix everything in it that's falling apart.

* * *

Sophie

I cannot believe that my mom knew all along about Dad and Dhanu

And right now she's still staring at me in disbelief after I just confessed that I stole the ring from her. Then went and lost the stupid thing. And I need to say this to her right now because it's practically pushing its way out of my mouth. And it's the perfect line too.

"Karma's a bitch huh, Mom. But you already knew that."

She looks a bit shocked for a split second, then she grins. "*Touché ma fille.* I guess I had it coming. So, any idea where the ring might be? I'd just like to send it back to her and move on."

"I might have a lead on getting it back. And no doubt you're moving on. Especially with that new fella in your life these days, huh?" Snap! Those words are so delicious on my tongue.

She is gobsmacked. "How...how do you already know about Sebastian?"

"Saw you with him at Sweetest Smoke, at lunch time yesterday. Jonah and I tried to get in, but there was a lineup. There you were in the window, head to head with some guy. *Kissing* in public. God, how gross. I was surprised when you agreed to order take-out from the same place for dinner."

Mom looks slightly amused at this news. And slightly lovestruck too. "Yeah, well I couldn't admit that I'd been there already yesterday, right? So, I just ordered something different from the menu." She touches my hand and sighs. Okay, so now you know. He's actually an old friend from high school that I reconnected with on Facebook. He started messaging me recently, and I brushed him off at first. I guess I was still in denial about your dad. What a dum-dum. Then after I caught them in a huge lie last month, I figured what the hell. You only live once. So, we've been seeing each other a lot over the last few weeks. And I think I really like him."

Mom looks happier than I've ever seen her look in I don't even know how long. She looks like a moonstruck teenager instead of a forty-something mom. I'm afraid to ask, but I know that I need to, so I can even begin to process all the family angst in my life.

"So...so what was this huge lie, anyway, Mom?" Do I really want to hear about this?

She sighs again, squeezes my hand. "What I did is pretty rotten and shameful," she says, not looking the least bit ashamed.

"After she told me that she had to go home and help take care of her ailing mom, I did a bit of snooping in her bedroom while she was at the market one day. Like I said, I already had a sneaking suspicion. I caught the way that your dad was always looking at her. You can't hide the light in your eyes when you're in love. I could tell he had it bad. I don't know how the actual physical part began, or when."

Just the thought of Dad making out with Dhanu makes me cringe. He must be nearly fifteen years older than her. Wow, what a dirt bag he is.

"Gross. I guess I missed that. But I probably wasn't looking for it either. I mean, Dhanu was like a sister to me. I trusted her, like a member of the family. She was with us for like ten years!"

"Right, and for most of that time everything was fine. Your dad tried his best for a while after that other incident years ago. You know, when I wound up on the psyche ward, long time coming. But it's a two-way street. Maybe she led him on, maybe it was the other way around. Doesn't matter. I started noticing last fall. And watching. And it was subtle at first. Until it wasn't anymore, and then I knew for certain."

"And so what did you find out when you snooped, Mom?"

"A plane ticket hidden in her drawer. For Amsterdam. Not Sri Lanka. So, I snooped on her phone, too. Found text messages from your dad. Very, shall we say, unsubtle ones. She never used a password for her phone. Guess she trusted me, too." Mom shrugs and smiles. "Getting this off my chest is actually such a huge relief. You can't even imagine."

It's my turn to sigh as all the puzzle pieces begin falling into place. "So, no wonder Dad has been away so much lately. Guess he'll be gone for good soon, huh?"

"He's already bought a condo downtown, honey. I've already confronted him, and basically kicked him out. We were going to tell you this weekend. When he gets home from Amsterdam with Dhanu, and she moves into his place with him. Your choice whether you go there to hang out with them or not."

"That probably won't be happening for a while, Mom. Because right now just the thought of it makes me sick right to my core. So, tell me about this Sebastian guy."

Mom can't hide the love light in her eyes. And her smile is wider than it's ever been.

"Sebastian is into all the same things as I am. We've gone to some plays. He belongs to a theatre group. I may join up if I can only find the courage. It's been a long haul, living with a dad like yours, you know. I've lost confidence in myself." She tears up for a second then starts blinking fast. "I haven't been able to trust him ever again. Luckily my head meds are working, or I would have crashed fast after the final stab in the heart when he took Dhanu away with him.”

“So, Sebastian’s already more of a soul mate than Dad ever was, huh Mom?” Mom smiles and nods. This seems as good a time as any to make a few more confessions to her. Right now she’s vulnerable and calm, and oozing with some newfound confidence.

Which maybe she’s had all along, and I should have noticed by now. Silly me.

“So, guess what Mom? We already knew about them, Jonah and I. He found a photo on Insta the other day, of the two of them in Amsterdam. Just sheer luck, really, six degrees of separation. And he isn’t taking it very well. He’s having what sounds like anxiety symptoms. I’m worried about him. I don’t want him to crash on us.”

Mom clutches her throat and her face sags. “Stupid social media. And poor Jonah. We’ll have to help him get on top of that ASAP.”

And right then Jonah steps into the kitchen doorway.

“No, you won’t,” he tells us. “Because now that I know the truth, I’m already starting to feel way better. It’s like a fog is lifting or something.”

His face is a mask of pain. He’s totally lying.

“You were there the whole time, weren’t you,” I say grinning at my brother, hoping to maybe get him to smile back. “Just hiding in the hallway eavesdropping on us. Stinker.”

"Pretty much. I snuck back down to listen to what you were talking about. Just in time to hear all about catching them in a 'huge lie'." He slowly sinks back onto the chair he abandoned. "And I want you to know that I support you in all this, Mom. Dad is a snake. I think I might even hate him. And I don't want to hate him, you know. It's just that he totally fucked our family over, and I'm not sure I'll ever be able to forgive him for that. Because, you know...he, he's just such a...piece of..." a ragged choking sob.

And then it happens. His face scrunches up, like it used to when he was a little boy. Tears start leaking down his cheeks. Then he buries his face in his hands and his shoulders start to shake as he sobs uncontrollably. Mom is on her feet in a flash. She glides around the table and engulfs him in her arms, kissing the top of his head, stroking his hair.

"I'm making a doctor's appointment for you, Jonah my love," she murmurs. "We need to get on top of this now, before you totally morph into me." Then she looks at me over Jonah's head. "Now, about this infamous ring, Sophie. How are you going to get it back for me, anyway. Because my ridiculous little 'steal the ring for revenge' plot isn't sitting so well anymore."

Jonah suddenly shrugs out of Mom's gentle grip. "Hang on a sec," he says. "Did I just hear right? You actually *stole* that ring from Dhanu after you found out about the two of them. And then told us she gave it to you?" My brother is as gobsmacked as I am, of course.

Mom looks something like contrite as she nods. "And I'm not proud of myself for doing it Jonah, believe me. I need to make it right."

"Yeah, your chin is on the floor right now, just like mine was, huh?" I can't help saying.

My brother half grins and nods as he swipes his tears away. "Wow, that is totally awesome, Mom," he says. "Best news I've heard all year."

"So, where's the ring," Mom asks me. "You maybe have a lead, you said, Sophie?"

"Yup, I'm pretty sure I do, Mom. And I promise I'm going to try and help you fix this ring thing. Once and for all so we can all move on. But please, can we eat now? It's already after nine!"

* * *

By Monday morning I know what I have to do next, because I promised Mom. After school today, I have to try to meet up with that girl who was, I'm pretty positive, about to ask me about the ring near the bus stop on Monday. I only hope it's not too late. Mom said we can offer her a $100 reward if she gives it back to us. Hope she still has it!

My family insanity right now is starting to affect every aspect of my life. I find it hard to concentrate on anything, like my head is in the clouds. As Mr. Mills actually mentioned in front of the whole class today. Twice apparently before I even heard him saying 'Hello! Earth to Sophie. Do you read me'. Which was excruciating when I snapped out of my daze. Even more so when my phone vibrated on my lap, and 'cloud', 'UFO' and 'alien' emojis plus LOLs from half of my friends popped up. Note to self: follow the rules and turn your phone off during class from now on—like nobody else does—so jerks can't chirp you.

Then, right after Math class when I check my phone, I find a few texts from Lexi. They're all in caps too.

NEED YOU TO MEET ME OUT BY THE GOALPOSTS AT LUNCH SOS

NEED YOU TO HELP ME FIGURE THIS OUT SOS

HELP ME! SOS

I text her back okay. And start wondering what the big new life-altering emergency will be this time. My needy friend has a habit of making everything about her anyway. So, her SOS texting is her way of manipulating the rest of her friend circle. She expects us all to come running whenever she beckons, so we can hear all the excruciating and usually boring details of whatever she thinks is messing up her plans.

I wonder how many of us will have to huddle together on the football field this time, to listen to her whine about how her parents won't let her have the car this weekend and one of us needs to step up. Or how she needs one of us to have an online shopping purchase delivered to our house, so her parents won't find out she used their credit card to place an order. Because, of course, her parents never check the actual bills each month anyway, but their front door camera would show a delivery being made. Blah blah blah.

Every time I almost feel sorry for her, she does something stupid and all that pity just fades away like her annual cottage summer suntan. I'm so done with her poor-me tales of woe. Nobody has perfect parents. Or perfect kids either, obviously. We all come with our own perception of how things should be. Or how we wish they could be. I mean, it's always so easy to blame your parents. But maybe sometimes you have to look inside yourself, too.

Hmm. Maybe I've actually learned something from writing this essay.

At lunch time I grab a chicken Caesar wrap from the cafeteria and hustle outside to meet up with Lexi. She's there ahead of me, standing in the cool April breeze, one arm wrapped around the goalpost as she stares at her phone screen. When she looks up and sees me coming, she definitely isn't smiling. Hmm. That could mean that she might actually have a real problem this time. And another clue is that none of her other so-called friends are out here to help solve her problem. Which is sort of a gut punch because it means that I'm the one who has to help her deal with whatever new dilemma is messing her up. Her oldest and closest friend who she always turns to first.

"So, what's up," I ask her in a casual voice so I don't feed into her SOS drama.

"Something bad might be happening," she tells me with an actual look of terror on her face this time. "Read this email and tell me what you think."

I take her phone and start reading aloud from the screen.

'Dear Ms. Hunter,

It has come to the attention of the administration that you might be offering assistance to your fellow students in the guise of helping them to revise their projects and assignments, when you are in fact actually completing the entire assignment for them. This goes for essays and lab reports as well as simple homework tasks. And also, that you might be accepting compensation for these unorthodox activities.

Please report to the principal's office after school today to discuss this matter. We hope that you can provide a reasonable explanation for what has occurred. We have faith in our students to do the right thing at all times, and to behave in a manner that is

It's signed by the principal. I read it twice. Then just stare at the screen in disbelief. It finally happened. Someone ratted her out. It's only taken the whole school year. She started her little enterprise back in September when her parents told her that they're cutting off some of her monthly allowance since she needs to get a job. She cooked up this scheme, told her folks she's being paid for tutoring. Yes, in so many ways Lexi is a huge brainiac genius. But sometimes it comes back to bite her in the ass. Like this time. At long last. I want to laugh out loud but keep a straight face.

"Oh no, Lexi. This is awful news. What do you think happened anyway?"

Tears are sliding down her face now, which keeps morphing between sad and angry. And I can't come anywhere close to feeling sorry for her. In fact, I'm revelling in this fiasco. Sadly.

"I'm not sure. Someone must have ratted me out or something. I trusted everyone, you know. I'm doing them a huge service. Helping them pass so they get good grades. We have to apply for university next year, you know. I'm just trying to help out the cause."

Give me a break! "Okay, so what does this have to do with me, anyway? I mean, it sucks that they're on to you. But you had to figure this would happen eventually. You haven't been very secretive. Everyone knows. You hand out business cards. Geez Lex. Seriously. Dumb move."

Lexi looks as if I just slapped her in the face. And maybe metaphorically, I did.

"Well, you're my best friend since grade school, Soph, so I though you would at least help me figure out a way to get through this."

"Like how exactly. You need to just go into the office and find out what happens next, right? I mean, I figure if you're lucky, you'll just get suspended, and not totally expelled."

"At least they haven't called my folks yet," Lexi says, frowning as she stares at her screen. "At least I'm not sure about that. What if my parents are there after school?"

"Sounds like a high chance of that happening," I admit as I start to unwrap my wrap. "It's too cool out here. I'm going back into the caf to eat."

"Wait!" She grabs my blazer sleeve. "I need you to come with."

"What? Where?" She can't possibly mean what I think she means, can she?

"To the office after school. To vouch for my character. To tell them how long we've known each other. And what a good friend I am to everyone. That I'm just trying to help out, almost like community service."

Hah! "Oh, I get it." I take a bite of my wrap and chew slowly, mulling this over as she stares at me in utter desperation. "So, what you're really saying is that you want me to lie for you."

"What are you talking about?" she says, stomping her expensive Prada boot. "Please, Sophie. I need you badly right now. You have to back me up on this. You need to do the right thing and help me out. Just like I've always done for you."

Again, hah! That's a bit of a stretch.

"Sorry, babe," I say with a shrug. "Not happening. You're on your own this time."

I turn around and walk away. First time I've done this in our entire friendship. For once Lexi needs to know what it feels like to fail at something. Someday she might chalk it all up as a lesson learned, no matter how much it's stinging her right now.

And right now, I've got way too much going on to spend one more second thinking about how screwed Lexi is going to be after school today. Right around the time I plan on meeting up with that girl and getting the ring back so Mom can find some closure. And so we can get Dhanu and her trail of misery out of our lives for good. Forever.

Chapter Nine

Tara

The next day at school, I keep to myself, avoid all my friends, and stay focused on my game plan. One that should help solve my problems and make me feel good and whole inside again.

Just before rehearsal is set to begin, Silas sidles up to me in the auditorium. "I thought things went great last night, didn't you? I can't wait to start rehearsing today."

"Um, yeah, that might not be happening, Silas," I tell him as his smile melts. Then I hurry over to the drama coach at centre stage before he can start asking any questions.

"There's something I need to say, Ms. Wilding. To you and the entire cast."

Ms. Wilding looks curious and confused. "Go ahead," she says, then claps her hands.

Everyone turns to face us, waiting for our director to give directions. She nods at me.

"Sorry to interrupt the rehearsal, everyone," I say. "But something has happened, a sort of family emergency, and circumstances in my life have suddenly changed, big time!"

Might as well be dramatic about it. From the corner of my eye, I spot Priya. She's totally focused on what I'm about to say. After avoiding me for so long, she's finally paying attention.

"Turns out," I continue, "that I just found out my mom and I have to move. This weekend! It's very unexpected, and extremely random, but it's happening fast, and I can't stop it. So, I have to spend the rest of this week helping to pack after school, every day. She needs me."

Murmurs from the cast and crew. My gaze drifts to Silas's face. He's frowning. He's not okay with this, and I'm sure that everything else I'm about to say is going to make things even worse.

"And so, I'm going to need someone to fill in for me all week, if that's okay Ms. Wilding. Next week I'll be back, but for the next few days I'll need my own understudy. The good news is, someone else knows the part as well as I do. That person is Priya." I point toward her, and she gasps. "She can be my understudy now that Iris is gone."

"Are you absolutely certain about this, Tara? Because you need the practice yourself. Production week is coming fast," Ms. Wilding says.

She does not look thrilled with me. I hate letting her down, but it has to happen for so many crazy reasons nobody can even imagine.

"Yes, I am. Like I just said, my mom needs me. I hope you understand how important it is for me to help her out with all the sorting and packing. It's a huge job."

"Excuse me, Ms. Wilding, I'm not sure I'm okay with this," Silas says in a tight voice. "I mean, Iris and I had this nailed, and now with this new setback..."

Our drama teacher holds up a hand to silence him. His face stiffens even more.

"And you really know the Emily part, Priya?" Ms. Wilding asks her. "Because even though Tara can't rehearse with us this week, it would be perfect if you can take over as understudy on such short notice."

Priya seems frozen in time for a second as her wide startled eyes lock on mine.

"I...well I...I'm not sure," Priya stammers as her eyes flicker next toward Silas. But when I look his way, he's staring at me with hard questions on his face.

"Priya, you know it's true. I've actually seen her lip syncing the 'Emily Webb' lines along with Iris," I tell the cast. "I think she knows just about everyone's part off by heart."

Priya stands there looking embarrassed, and I know for sure she's blushing.

Ms. Wilding's face softens. "I hope the move goes smoothly, Tara. And Priya, I need an answer right now, because otherwise I'll have to make other arrangements."

Now Priya is staring at me like a frightened rabbit. "Say yes," I tell her. "You know you can do this. It's just for a few days. It'll be a huge help to me."

She lets out a sigh. "Okay then," she says, nodding, smiling at Silas. "I'll do it. Hope that's okay with you, Silas."

"It's... it's good. It's fine. I'm sure it will work out great. Let's get started." But he doesn't sound as if he sincerely means it. He's been counting on me to do a great job, rehearse like mad to be ready for production week. And now I'm letting him down.

Silas looks so disappointed that I have to turn away. I hope he won't be angry for too long. But it's only for a few days. And now Priya has her chance in the spotlight. In Silas's spotlight too. She can try to get as close as she wants to this guy she's crushing on. In fact, now she'll even get to kiss him. I leave the school running, gulping air, letting the cool breeze wash over my face and the warm spring sunshine soothe me like a gentle balm.

"Mission part one, accomplished," I murmur as I set off running. "Now for part two."

There's a bus stop bench right near the spot where I had the run-in with that girl in her school uniform yesterday. That's where I sit down and open a novel. I plan on waiting it out, hoping she might show up at some point again today. That moonstone ring is practically throbbing in my pocket. It needs to be gone from my life.

And sure enough, 'round about four thirty, a transit bus trundles to a stop. The door hisses open and she steps out and glances my way.

"Hello again," I say when our eyes lock. "I think we need to talk, don't we?"

Her pretty face explodes into a smile. "Thank God you're here," she says. "I'm Sophie, and I need what you have. And I can even offer you a reward. This is more than urgent."

She sits down beside me and offers me her hand, which I shake. As if we're making a pact or something.

"I'm Tara. And I agree. Thank God *you're* here. I need to get rid of this crazy thing."

I dig the ring out of my pocket and touch her arm. "Please, I beg of you. Take this insane ring back. I can't stand to look at it anymore. I don't even need a reward. Just make it gone for good from my life!"

"No reward? Guess I'll give the money back to my mom then. Ugh, you know I used to love that ring, but now I can't stand the sight of it." She plucks it from my fingers. Holds it at arm's length away from her as if it's poison or something, looks away as if the ring might burn her retinas. "You wouldn't even believe the whole pile of dung that revolves around this stupid ring."

"Oh yeah? Try me," I tell her. "Because ever since I found it, my life has pretty much turned completely upside down. That thing is jinxed or hexed or something. I swear!"

"Wow, do tell," Sophie says. "Wait. Why don't you come over to my house. I live close by. I can make us a k-cup of coffee. Whatever flavour you want. And that ring, well it kind of belongs to my mom, and there's a really good reason she needs to get rid of it herself."

Hmmm. I know Mom needs me to help her pack, but right now hearing Sophie's story is more important, and I'm actually just way too curious, and need to find out more.

"Sure, lead the way," I say, then fall in step beside her as she starts talking.

"So right up until I lost it last Friday, that ring sort of belonged to my mom. She told my brother and me that it was a gift. From our nanny, before she had to go back to Sri Lanka to look after her sick 'amma'. But ever since last week when I stole it from my mom, then I wound up losing it, everything in our life has totally changed."

"Wow, seriously?" I swallow hard. "Changed in what way?" This is getting way too weird. How can we have so much in common when the two of us have never even met in our lives.

"Coming to that," she says. "So, I lost the ring last week when I was rushing home for the dumbest reason ever, that I don't want to even think about anymore. I panicked when

I realized the moonstone ring was missing, and retraced my steps to look for it, knowing my mom would freak out. But of course, you had it by then, I guess. So, I put up the signs on Saturday morning."

I figure I might as well come clean right away. "I must have picked the ring up right after you lost it. I thought it was beautiful, mesmerizing. To be honest, I wanted to hang onto it a bit longer after I found out that moonstones might have special powers. So, I tore your signs down. Believe me, I regretted it right away. Which is why I put up new ones. But you never called me."

Sophie stops dead on the sidewalk, grabs my shoulders and stares into my eyes.

"You have *got* to be kidding me. I did the same thing with the signs *you* made, Tara."

"Come on!" I yelp. "Why did you do that?"

"Because I wasn't sure I ever wanted to find it again. I ripped down the signs, shredded them and put them in the recycle bin."

By then I'm bent over laughing. "I ripped your signs into tiny pieces and flushed them all down the toilet," I admit. And suddenly we're standing there screaming laughing at the insanity of this whole ridiculous thing.

Then we're turning a corner onto a very familiar street. And walking up to a very familiar house, and for a scary second I think we might be going to that house. But no, we're going to the one next door. And someone is out in the driveway next to Sophie's, bouncing a basketball.

And that someone is Silas Symonds. Gah!

"You've got to be joking. You live next door to Silas Symonds?" I gasp.

"Oh, so that's his last name, huh? Sure do," she says, grinning. "I saw you going over there on Sunday. And I figured he'd be out here bouncing. You have no idea how crazy that bouncing sound is starting to make me now. I need it to stop, or I'll lose it completely!"

When Silas sees us coming mid-toss, he smiles and waves, then he freezes, as shocked and confused as I am that we're seeing each other right here, right now. And the basketball nails him right in the head, then goes bouncing away. Ouch.

"What are you even doing here, Tara?" he asks me in an accusing voice. Ugh. Awkward. Because of course I'm supposed to be home right now, helping my mom pack. Family emergency, etcetera.

"It's a long story and hard to explain, to be honest," I tell him. By his stiff expression, he clearly isn't convinced. "Hope the rehearsal went okay. Wait, why are you even home from rehearsing so early?"

"I bailed," he says with a shrug. "After your big announcement I felt like shit and I left early. Had a lot of thinking to do."

Sophie is giving us both the side-eye, clearly assessing the situation.

"Join us for a coffee, Silas," she says, then links her arms in ours and leads us both inside. "You two need to talk, it seems. I'm going upstairs to get changed. Be right back."

Silas and I stand beside the gleaming granite countertop in Sophie's kitchen. This house is even more amazing than Silas's place. But right now, there's a strange awkwardness. Because so much is hanging in the air like a choking smoke. Silas and I didn't leave school today on the best of terms. I feel as if he doesn't even want to meet my eyes because he's so disappointed in how I let him down when he was depending on me. Thank God Sophie is a quick change artist, back in about three minutes.

She sets out the coffee pods. I choose a mocha latte, and Silas reaches for a dark roast. Sophie picks a hazelnut for herself. She takes three beautiful flowered ceramic mugs from the cupboard. Wow, they all match too. The whole time the coffee machine is humming, we all just stand there, waiting for someone to say something. When each of us is finally holding a steaming mug, Sophie sits on one of the tall red leather counter stools, and Silas and I follow her lead.

An uncomfortable silence muffles the room. We're all facing forward at the counter, Sophie between Silas and me, which is helpful. Just being in the same rooms as Silas right now, after I've apparently turned his acting life upside down, is breaking my spirit even more. I can almost feel his angry vibes crackling in the air.

"Okay, you two. Just say something, for the love of God," Sophie tells us. "Why were you at his place on Sunday, for one thing, Tara? Were you helping him study or run lines or what?"

Silas narrows his eyes. "How did you even know about that, Sophie?"

"I heard Tara knocking and I peeked out," Sophie admits. "I hear every single thing that happens out in your driveway, since our houses are so close together." She cringes a little. "And sometimes I just happen to look outside at the right moment and see things that I don't really need to see." She cringes even more.

What's that supposed to mean, I wonder.

"What's that supposed to mean," Silas asks with a bit of a frown.

"Long story," Sophie tells him. "So, you were there why, Tara?" she asks me again.

"We were rehearsing for a play. Our Town. The Emily and George roles," I explain.

"Ah, okay, now I get it. Oh, so you're Emily Webb in the play. Silas was telling me all about it, on Saturday evening at Starbucks. Great play, by the way," Sophie says. "I saw it with my school at the Shaw Festival a couple of years ago. So, what seems to be the problem, then."

Huh? Wait. Sophie was at Starbucks?

"Wait, what now? You were there too on Saturday? At Starbucks?" I ask her.

"Yep, I knew when we ran into each other at the bus stop that I'd seen you somewhere before. I saw that fight you had with your friend too. When she stomped out all mad. And then you left a while later. So, I went over and joined Silas at his table and helped him rehearse."

"Wow," I say, shaking my head. "Major crazy coincidences happening here. And yet another long story," I tell her, then blow on my latte and take a quick sip to avoid Silas's troubled eyes.

"I'm starting to think there aren't any coincidences. It's like our whole lives have been spinning toward this very moment in time when we're all sitting together at this counter. Seems so weirdly random, yet not. Come on you guys," Sophie prods us. "Let's clear the air once and for all, okay?"

Silas clears his throat. His whole face is a scowl. "Okay I'll start. So, Tara. When you made your big announcement after school today, it felt as if you were letting down the entire production with a sort of crap excuse. Some of us talked about it and decided to give you the benefit of the doubt. We trusted that you'd be back in time next week. And that you'll keep rehearsing your lines, somehow or other. And now, well, here you are! Weren't you supposed to be helping out your..."

"My mom to pack for our house move. Yes, I was, Silas. But there's this problem with a moonstone ring that had to be solved first. Sophie, if you wouldn't mind presenting the evidence that will help to absolve me of a certain perceived crime. And maybe even to regain the trust of my fellow cast member. Who has taught me so much about acting, that I'll be eternally grateful to him."

A hint of a smile crosses Silas's face and he nods. Cool! I think maybe he's starting to forgive me. Sophie places the ring on the counter and we all sit there staring at it.

"Nice ring," Silas says. "Whose is it anyway?"

"And that's where this whole story starts," Sophie says.

Then we both begin explaining the ridiculous twisted tale.

* * *

Sophie

Tara spends a few minutes explaining the story of how she found the ring near the bus stop, and every crazy thing that's changed in her life since then. Silas and I sit in shocked silence as she tells us about how her mom won a lottery and hooked up pretty

219

much permanently with some guy she met on a dating app. On the exact same day she found the ring on the sidewalk last week. Was it luck or fate, how this all so randomly happened, she keeps repeating. And if it wasn't for me losing and her finding the ring, the three of us wouldn't even be sitting together right here, right now. It's as if a whole series of 'sliding door moments' brought us all together, she tells us.

Next, I start my own version of the story about how by sheer dumb luck a moonstone ring brought all three of us together at this kitchen counter at this particular moment in time. Each of us continues staring straight ahead as we sip our coffees. From time to time, I turn my head in one direction then the other to gauge their reactions. Both Silas and Tara seem completely caught up in my bizarre tale of our dad's deception with our nanny, how Jonah found the incriminating photo on Instagram, and how my mom—who already knew the truth—decided to steal the ring from Dhanu for revenge. That comes as a bit of a shock to both of them.

"So, I guess you come by it honestly," Tara says with an undisguised snicker. "First your mom steals the ring from your nanny as payback, and then you steal it from your mom for spite, or some strange distraction technique or whatever."

"Bingo," says the mostly silent Silas, then lets out a bit of a chuckle after Tara's cutting comments that I so deserved. "That whole apple not falling far from the tree analogy."

"Sounds like the plot of some crazy-ass Netflix series," Tara adds.

"Wow, we've barely even met, you guys, and you're both already chirping me? Oh well, whatever. *Om mane padme hum.*" Finger circles, seeking grounding and peace. I know they're both staring at me, but I keep my eyes closed and say it again. "*Om mane padme hum.*"

"I'm not even going to ask," Tara says.

"Ancient Buddhist mantra," Silas says without skipping a beat. "My aunt and her wife use it all the time during their meditation sessions. Sometimes I even sit in with them. I'm finding meditation helps keep me grounded and focused. Reduces stress too."

"So, hang on a sec," I interrupt him as a lightbulb switches on inside my brain. "That's who you live with? Your aunt and her wife? I've never even seen them. They always drive their cars straight into the garage when they get home."

"To keep the snow off in winter. But now, so I can shoot hoops. That's another form of meditation for me. Like I was telling you the other day, Sophie. Helps keep me focused."

I could say something right now. This is my chance to admit to Silas that the relentless bouncing ball under my window is breaking my brain. But I don't want to distract him. I need to find a subtle way to ask more questions about what the situation is next door. Time to drag my stool around to the other side of the counter so I can sit face to face with these two people who have so suddenly landed in my life.

"I met Hazel and Maggie on Sunday," Tara tells me. "They're really nice. So how come you don't live with your parents anyway, Silas."

Okay, so subtlety is not necessarily a necessity I guess. Tara seems to be so open and real compared to some of the other girls I know. No head games. I really admire that. Plus, she seems super funny. And can even laugh at herself, too. And wait. Silas lives with two women? Hmm.

"Thought you'd never ask," Silas says with a sigh. He scrapes his fingers through his dark wavy hair. His face is solemn, his coffee-coloured eyes deeply troubled. I think I know what's coming next. "Long story short, my mother hates that I'm gay, and it's breaking my dad's heart."

Tara chokes then spurts a mouthful of coffee across the counter. The spray hits me right in the exact same spot as the chocolate milk did the other day. And boom! Guess what? I'm wearing the exact same top, too. The silky cream-coloured yoga top that I inherited from my mom after ruining it.

"Oh God, sorry, Sophie," Tara says, grabbing for the roll of paper towels on the counter. She rips some pieces off, hands a bunch to me, then starts wiping up the puddle in front of her.

"Hey, isn't that the same top you were wearing when you sprayed chocolate mi..."

"Yes, it is, Silas. And I almost had that stain out after multiple washings too, dammit. Oh sorry, Tara, that's okay, no worries. Let me just soak these paper towels in cold water and blot the coffee out of it real quick. So, something tells me you had no idea Silas was gay, huh?"

At this point Tara's face looks like it's on fire. Which I totally understand. Apparently we were sisters in the unrequited love of a gay guy. It is such a ridiculous coincidence that I feel like laughing out loud. Instead, I let the two of them figure things out for themselves.

"Um, well, I actually think every little thing is starting to fall into place." Tara is gazing at Silas in a strange, confused way right now, and he has the widest smile on his face.

"Wait a minute, Tara. You don't mean to tell me that you had no clue, until right this *second*, that I'm totally gay? And you were actually CRUSHING on me?"

Sprawling across the countertop, Tara buries her face in her arm and her shoulders start to shake. Crying? Or laughing? Or a little of both? Then she throws her head back and starts shrieking laughing between gasps for air. Her laugh is so sweet and silly and contagious that I crack up too.

"I think I started to catch on when we were rehearsing at your place. Since, when I had to kiss you in the wedding scene, I felt absolutely nothing," she says. "Like kissing a cousin or something. No spark. No...uh, primal urges, if you know what I mean. I thought it was just me, that I suck at acting. But nope. Whew. What a relief."

"Huh I actually thought I did a pretty good job of faking it." He shrugs and laughs. "I mean, I've never even kissed a girl. Unlike Katy Perry. So that was a total stretch for me."

"And unlike when you and Zeke were making out beside the garage the other day," I say to him with a wink. "Now it's my turn for a confession. I was madly crushing on you. As you might have already figured out from the front porch fiasco. Until I saw you guys going at it out there."

"So, you've been spying on me, huh Sophie," he says. God, if he only knew how much! "Wow, I totally missed all that," he tells us. "Imagine! So many beautiful, available ladies madly in love with me and I'm completely oblivious. And wouldn't care anyway."

"Oh, you have absolutely no idea," Tara tells him. "In fact, when this becomes common knowledge, there will be a whole parade of broken hearts at school, trust me. But then again, quite a few of the guys will probably be thrilled to find out."

Silas's eyes light up when he hears that news. Yep, definitely a player.

"Okay, so now that we've cleared the air, what's going on with your family, Silas?" I ask him. "Why does your mom hate that you're gay? I mean, that's a total heartbreaker, dude. What century is she stuck in anyway? She needs to catch up with the times."

"Right?" Tara agrees. "It's not like it's your fault or anything."

"Oh no, of course not, according to my mom. She says it's my dad's fault. Because his sister, my Aunt Hazel, is gay. Figures it's hereditary." Silas sighs and shuts his eyes. "Can you imagine what living in that situation was like? The two of them started arguing the second I came out when I turned seventeen. I couldn't take it anymore, felt like it was all my fault. Even briefly questioned the possibility my mom was right, then gave my head a shake. There is NO gay gene, as much as Mom so desperately wants to believe there is one. Turns out it's just a happy-for-me, unhappy-for-mom, weird-ass family coincidence."

"Wow, so cool that your aunt is letting you stay with them," Tara says. "And in a pretty sweet neighbourhood, too."

"Yep, I got lucky. They moved into their big house over the winter. Lots of space for me and all the room a kid takes up. Got the whole basement to myself. I miss my family, though."

"That's so messed. Tara and I thought we had family issues. But this is…it's just so wrong," I tell him as anger sizzles inside of me. "We need to do something to help you, Silas. Your mom needs to get educated, open her mind."

"Hah," he says with a loud snort. "Good luck with that. Her mind is very narrow. She comes from an even narrower background. It's hard to escape what's basically been bred into your bones."

"So, is she planning on coming to see the play?" Tara asks him. "Has she ever seen you perform? Does she have any idea how amazing you are?"

Silas's eyes are downcast. "She associates stage acting with queerness," he admits. In the saddest voice I've heard from him yet. "She's been so brainwashed. Thinks every playwright is Oscar Wilde."

"Wow I can't even imagine being that narrow," I tell him. "My mom has a theatre background. And you know what? I've decided I'm coming to see your play and I'm bringing her along. She will absolutely love it. Probably knows all the lines, too."

"Cool," Silas says. "I'd love that. And I'd love to meet your mom too."

And right that second my phone vibrates on the counter beside me, and the screen lights up. It's a text from Lexi.

"One moment please," I tell Tara and Silas. "Bit of school drama happening right now. My friend Lexi might be expelled for cheating. She was getting paid for doing essays and assignments for other kids at school. Gotta check. Uh oh. Not good." I read the words out loud, wondering for a split second if maybe I feel sorry for her. Nope. Not this time.

Two week suspension. Thanks for your support. Asshole jerk :/

"Well, my oldest friend is now officially screwed," I tell them.

"Wow, harsh words," Tara tells me, wide eyed. "With friends like that..."

"Right? I've been thinking that for a while now. Frenemy is a word for a reason. And I guess maybe our friendship has officially ended now. Oh well. It's been on the way out for a long time anyway. What's wrong with you, Silas? Why do you have that weird look on your face."

Silas half smirks, like he's fighting off an outright laugh.

"Uh, well, hmm. How to put this. My friend Zeke is kind of a stickler for rules. Cheats make him all kinds of crazy. He busts his butt for good marks and hates that not everyone else thinks the same way. He might have ratted out your friend after she gave him her card. I can't be sure, but he just about freaked out in the driveway after she left. Would not stop talking about it. I had to kiss him just to shut him up!"

"Wow, sucks to be Lexi, doesn't it," Tara says to me. "She met her match, finally."

"You know I even kept on warning her, but she would *not* listen," I tell them, feeling wistful for a moment. It really isn't easy to watch your oldest friend crash and burn this way. "Said it was just like an academic service for students. Guess she finally gave her business card to the wrong person."

"So, it would seem," Silas says. "Truth is, I already ended it with Zeke. Figured out he's kind of a whiner. Somewhat of a drama queen. And he lives too far away, so now we're just friends. Time to move on. New places, new faces."

"Know something," Tara says. "I'm really glad you're gay, Silas. Because if you were cisgender, and Sophie and I were still madly crushing on you, it wouldn't end well. We'd have this big cat-fight competition, and then realize that you're kind of a player, and really not the best choice of potential boyfriends."

I toss my head back and start laughing along with Tara. "We sure got lucky this time, didn't we, girlfriend," I tell her. "And no thanks to this ridiculous moonstone ring, either."

"Ouch," he says, then laughs and shrugs. "Look, I'm kind of new at this whole dating thing. I got a late start, and I have a ton of catching up to do. It took too long before I admitted who I really was."

"Oh, trust me, we know who you really are, Silas," Tara tells him, and we all crack up.

"You know what's super weird in all this though," I tell Tara. "It's that we've been sort of living these parallel lives. Lots of frustration because of our thoughtless dads and our poor moms who have to suffer because of it. It's like we're so different, yet..."

"Yet so the same!" Tara blurts out. "I've been thinking the exact same thing. We've just been living our lives, struggling to do our best with all our different challenges. All of these bizarre coincidences we share. And then that hexed moonstone ring brings us together! As if we were meant to find each other all along. As if the two of us were meant to be hanging out together, along with Silas now, too. Oh sorry, that sounds really presumptuous. Wow, I need to just shut up!"

I can't help but start laughing as Tara stumbles over her words, blushing like crazy. Then Silas starts chuckling too. She's such a funny girl. It's nice to be laughing so much for a change. And just as I'm about to tell her that I could use some refreshing new friends in my life these days, there's a racket at the front door. It's Hurricane Frances making landfall. But there are two voices. And one's a man. Hmm. This could get interesting.

"Prepare yourselves," I warn my two friends. "My diva mom just blew in. And you might never be ready for this!"

Mom swirls into the room with her new/old boyfriend Sebastian. Now this guy looks more her type. Instead of the buttoned-down banker type like Dad, with trim hair and trim suits and trim everything, Sebastian's hair is a bit shaggy with touches of grey at the temple. He's wearing cool tortoise-shell glasses. And jeans, and Keds sneakers, and a vintage Beatles t-shirt.

"Hello everyone!" Mom says in a delighted voice. She's always loved an impromptu shindig. Any reason is a good one for lighting candles and opening wine. "Sebastian, this is my daughter, Sophie. And these are her friends, Silas, who lives next door. And…" She frowns at Tara for a second. "Oh, sorry honey. I don't think we've met. I'm Frances McMillan."

"Hi, I'm Tara," she says, shaking Mom's hand. Wow, I love Tara's wide open smile.

"Using your maiden name already, huh Mom?" I ask her.

"I'm ready to move on, Sophie," she says. She plants a quick kiss on her beau's cheek. He smiles, almost bashfully, and nods at us. Then her sparkling eyes spy the moonstone ring glinting on the countertop.

"Well, well, well," she says, picking it up. "Where did you come from, my pretty?"

Chapter Ten

Tara

Sophie's mom and her boyfriend just sit there staring at us in complete disbelief as we explain the bizarre random connections in this whole screwy ring thing. And how we've all wound up sitting together here at the kitchen counter today. But Frances and Sebastian crack up the most when we tell them about the two sets of each other's signs that we both tore down from lampposts and ripped into tiny pieces. Even Silas is shaking his head in confusion by then.

"Wow, that's seriously messed up," he says. "It's mind boggling, really."

"Oh, for the good old, bad old, high school days," Sebastian says with a pensive look in his eyes. "These two girls and their rollercoaster lives, and wild choices sure makes my own life seem bland and boring by comparison. How about you, Silas?"

"Um, I can't say that I totally agree with that, Sir," Silas tell him. "Being that these two lovely girls have both been dying to jump my bones, having no clue that I'm actually gay."

We all have a laugh over that one. Cringey laughs for Sophie and me, of course.

"So, what are you going to do with the ring now? Give it back to the nanny? And admit what you did?" I ask Sophie's mom.

"I've been thinking about that a lot over the last few days since it went missing. The guilt is really getting to me now. Especially since Sebastian and I have reconnected. So, I made a move."

There's a shuffling sound in the kitchen doorway, and when I look around, there's a guy standing there. He's crazy cute with a mess of sandy curls and probing green eyes. He looks a bit nervous, half smiling, half frowning, as if he isn't quite sure how he's feeling. Then his green eyes meet mine for a second, and he raises his eyebrows slightly like he's almost saying hello. He almost smiles a bit more, which almost looks promising. He reminds me a little of a younger Michael Cera.

"Oh hey, hi," I murmur. "I'm Tara Watson." He waves at me. I really like his smile.

"Hey. I'm Jonah," he tells me. "Welcome to the madhouse."

"Well look who showed up late to the party," Sophie says. "Were you eavesdropping out in the hallway as usual, Jonah?"

"Just for a few seconds," he admits, his narrowed eyes locked on Sebastian now. "So, what's the story here, anyway?"

Sounds skeptical, like he doesn't really want to find out.

"Jonah, honey! There you are! I was just going to call you to come meet this guy!"

Frances hurries over and tries to hug him in a whirl of scarves and a rattle of bracelets as he tries to duck out of her grasp. She's like some funky neo-hippie flower child or something.

"This is my friend Sebastian I've been telling you about," she says, almost breathless with joy. "He and I have reconnected, as you already know."

For an instant I think Sophie's brother might make a run for it, but instead he takes a deep breath.

"Hey there," Jonah says, then shuffles over to shake Sebastian's hand. "Nice to meet you. So, are you going to be our brand new jackass dad now, or what?"

Ouch! Even I can't help gasp at that admirable cutting line. When I look around, everyone else's face is frozen in shock as well. Talk about awkward. This guy is clearly hurting, though. His chin is trembling, his nostrils flaring. The only one who hasn't really reacted is Sebastian. He smiles in a gentle way at Jonah, then shakes his head a little.

"Look, Jonah, I'm not here to replace anyone. And I'm definitely not here to hurt anyone. I'm just here because your mom and I care a lot about each other. She asked me to come over so I could finally meet you two kids. Honestly, she never stops talking about how great you are. And let me tell you, she did a lot of soul searching before this moment could even happen."

"It's true," Frances tells her son. "I know how troubling all of this is to both of you. It's a crushing blow. But it's been in the stars for a long time. You both knew that, right?"

Sophie shrugs and nods. Jonah just rolls his eyes and mutters 'whatever'.

"I'm sorry if I upset you today, Jonah, and you too, Sophie," Sebastian tells them. "If you want, if this is making you and Sophie too uncomfortable, I can leave right now."

This guy is being so honest and genuine. Even Jonah notices. He stands there blinking slowly for a few seconds. Seems he's been totally taken by surprise, probably didn't expect such a gracious response to his zinger. He lets out a slow soft sigh.

"Uh, no, that's okay, I guess. You can stay. Sorry for being so rude."

"You know something Jonah," Sebastian says. "That went far better than I expected it would. I was honestly a little worried about possibly getting punched in the face. And I've been called far worse than a jackass in the past."

When everyone laughs a little at that line, the tension in the room starts to lift. And then it's suddenly too silent. Maybe I can help out with this awkward situation myself somehow.

"So, in case you're wondering, Jonah," I tell him, pointing at the ring on the counter. "I'm the unfortunate finder of the moonstone ring."

"Aha. The mysterious touchstone of this strange series of family 'affairs'," Jonah says making air quotes.

"Snap! Well said, brother of mine," Sophie tells him. "That's almost poetic."

"I've actually been saving that line, even practicing it," Jonah admits, which makes us all laugh, and helps to pop the angst bubble floating in the room. This guy is a special kind of a sweetie.

"And I'm Silas, your neighbour. We met in the driveway before."

"Right, I knew that already. Welcome to the 'hood," Jonah says. "So, is it cool if I shoot some hoops with you sometime?"

"Sure," Silas tells him. "Feel free to use it whenever. Even if I'm not out there."

"Sweet," Jonah says, as the shadow of a real smile finally crosses his face. Crazy cute.

"Perfect," Sophie says in a fake happy voice. Because it clearly isn't anywhere near perfect. She'll need to invest in a really good set of noise-cancelling headphones to escape the endless bouncing sound that's making her crazy. I have to stifle a snicker when our eyes meet, and she rolls hers in an exaggerated message of lost hope.

"So, continue, Mom," Sophie says. "You were going to tell us about some move you made, just before Jonah showed up. Should we be nervous about hearing whatever it is?"

"What's left to be nervous about," Jonah murmurs. "Every nasty thing has already happened. It's not going to get any worse than it already is, right Mom?"

He looks as if he might be about to cry again. I have a feeling that Jonah is experiencing anxiety big time over this, and I get it. Poor guy. I feel like hugging him now.

"Jonah, we have lots to talk about. But this isn't the time or place. Right now, all I'm talking about is this mesmerizing ring." She holds it up so the diamonds sparkle under the countertop lighting. The moonstone shimmers, and practically glows like a full moon. Wow, if I were a crow I'd be cawing. Love that beautiful bling ring. "So, I emailed Dhanu and confessed that I stole it, after letting her believe that she'd misplaced it before she left here last month."

"And how did that work out for you, Mom," Sophie asks her. "I mean, I know I'm guilty of the same crime, but I wouldn't have had to steal it from you to try and distract you, if you hadn't snatched it from her in the first place and started acting all weird and obsessive about it."

"Right you are," Frances tells Sophie. "Because of the guilt stress. And guess what. Dhanu doesn't even want it back. She says that it's tainted now. And will likely have bad juju forever."

Jonah snorts. "What's that supposed to mean?" he says.

"Like having bad luck associated with it," Sebastian explains. "She must figure that bad things will happen to anyone who owns it now. Superstitions, etcetera. And totally bunk of course."

"Yeah, well all I know is that ever since I started hearing about Dhanu's stupid jinxed ring, everyone and everything I thought I could trust and believe in has turned to crap. I never want to see that thing again. It only reminds me of the way everything used to be around here." He folds him arms up tight against his chest.

"Yeah, well you're kind of in denial, Jonah," Sophie tells him in a gentle voice. "But you can't possibly deny that we've seen this coming for a long time. Remember how you'd sneak into my room at night to ask me if everything was okay with Mom and Dad. You could see it coming years ago when Mom was being treated for her breakdown."

"Well then why does it feel like everyone's cheating on each other right now?" Jonah asks the whole room in a desperately sad voice. "I swear I have no clue who anybody in my family even is anymore. What is happening with us?"

"Don't believe your brain," Sophie tells her brother. "It's messing with your head right now. It's trying to take you back to a place that doesn't exist anymore."

"It's true, Jonah. People believe what they need to believe, retreat to their own comfort zone maybe," Frances tells them. "It helps with survival. Look kids, it's over between your dad and me. I'm not cheating on him. I'm just taking my life back after he spent so many years messing it up. We were way too immature when we got married. I knew what he was like going in, and he keeps proving that he'll never change. So, I made the decision for us. Why do you think he's away so much? We're staying friends though, even when the separation papers get signed and eventually a divorce comes through. We just absolutely cannot be married to each other anymore." Her green eyes flash with something like passion and confidence.

"Wow, talk about being honest with your kids," I can't help but blurt out. "Oops. Did I say that out loud." I offer them a half smile. "I really admire that. I wish my parents had split up as graciously as yours, Sophie and Jonah. You can't even imagine our nightmare. Which might finally be ending, fingers crossed."

"Yet my parental nightmare continues," Silas says with downcast eyes. Poor Silas. Maybe someday soon his mother will come around and accept him for who he truly is.

"So sorry about venting in front of guests," Frances says, with a namaste of her hands. "But this has been bottled up for so long." She taps her heart with her open palm. "Bottom line, I'm stuck with this ring now, and I don't really want it either. Since I can't undo the fact that I stole it for spite. What about you, Sophie? Would you like to have it?"

Sophie tilts her head like she's mulling the idea over for a second, then she winces.

"I stole it for spite too," she admits. "Distraction spite. Because you were so obsessed with it, acting as if it was changing your luck. Which was so dumb, it was making me nuts. So how about you, Tara? Finders keepers? You can have it if you want to take the risk." She grins at me, in an almost devious way.

What? "Seriously?" I say in complete disbelief as Frances nods her approval.

"Here, take it." Frances presses the ring into the palm of my hand. "Maybe some of its supposed luck will rub off on you."

"Wow, thanks, I think." I grin at them all then gaze at the object that started all this.

God, I love this gorgeous moonstone ring. As it glints in my hand, I consider all the possibilities. Both positive and negative. But maybe Dhanu is right, and it truly is jinxed now because of all the bad juju associated with it. Then again, so much has changed in my own life since I found it. Mom won the lottery and found a new guy, and we're moving out of our dump.

Plus, I get to play the part of Emily. So weird and random. And I actually did what I've wanted to for so long, hoofed my jerk of a dad when he was pissing me off, which he's been doing for way too long, and so deserved the other day. His blind rages made our life so miserable in the past that we even had to seek help from the women's shelter. We stayed there for a month until he lured mom back with his fake charm and false promises. Thank God, those days are done.

So, was it luck or fate, finding this moonstone ring? Did something mystical really happen, or was our lousy lifestyle just about to change anyway? Who can even know? But as much as the ring means everything nasty and negative to Sophie's family, whenever I look at it now, I see a shiny reminder of all the positive changes in my life that happened since finding it, whether just a coincidence or not. And I'm sure if Sophie's brother really stops and thinks hard about the way things have unfolded for them, he'll realize that everything has changed for the better in their lives too.

Just then Silas plucks the ring from the palm of my hand and has a good close look at it himself. As he turns it from side to side under the hanging pendant lights, the cut facets of the shoulder diamonds glitter as the moonstone glows in its shimmering mystical way.

"What's with this thing anyway, that makes you want to stare at it. *Look at that moon. Potato weather for sure.*" Silas murmurs.

"*Quite a moon!*" I say to Silas in reply. When we realize everyone is staring at us we start to laugh. "Quotes from *Our Town*," I explain. "Lots of moon imagery in the play."

Just then my cell phone chimes with a text message. When I check, it's my mom.

Where r u? thought we were packing 2gether?

Yikes!

OMW I text right back. I've been wanting to text that message forever. Now I finally can yay!

"Oh shoot," I tell everyone. "I'm way too late. Gotta run. I hope you guys get everything sorted out. So, I can really take this ring? You're absolutely sure about it?"

"Take it!" Frances, Sophie and Jonah yell in one voice.

"OMG, thanks!" I yell back. As the whole room cracks up, I make a dash for the door.

Out front I realize there's commotion in the driveway at Silas's place. A woman is crying, while Hazel and Maggie try to comfort her. They offer a quick wave, then walk the woman toward Sophie's front door.

No time to find out what's going on though. OMW home.

* * *

Sophie

"Wow, I'm so glad that creepy ring is gone for good," I tell everyone sitting around the counter. "Nice of my new friend Tara to take it off our hands. And she didn't even want the reward money for finding it."

My mom frowns for an instant, which she hasn't been doing as often the last few days.

"Actually, that money has already been designated for the cause. I feel like Tara really needs to take the hundred dollars as well, to clear the air of all the negativity associated with the ring."

"Seriously, Mom?" Jonah says, shaking his head. "A bit over the top, don't you think?"

"Our mom a bit over the top? I mean, when does that ever happen?" I tell my brother, stifling the laughter that's bubbling up in my throat. But too late, Jonah and I crack right up. Sebastian and Silas start laughing then too, and Mom just shrugs and sighs.

"I'll be happy to take the dough off your hands, though," Jonah adds with a snicker. "I'm more than willing to take that risk."

"Wait, what if we did something else with it," I tell them all with a quick finger snap. "Like how about if we, say, donate it to the mental health unit at the hospital that helped you out with your mental illness eight years back. That would take care of all the ring negativity, wouldn't it?"

Silence for a moment, then everyone starts nodding.

"I like that idea, Sophie," she says. "In fact, I like it very much. Especially since the two of us played a part in this whole lost-and-found ring debacle. I'll e-transfer some money to their donation fund later. Let's say we round it up to five hundred dollars for good measure."

"Sweet. It makes so much sense, Mom," I tell her, feeling something like pride for even coming up with the idea. It's almost like another step toward living in the moment.

"Funny thing, though," Mom says with a mysterious smile. "If you hadn't taken that ring from me, then gone and lost it, you'd have never even met Tara in the first place, am I right?"

"I've thought of that already," I admit. "So, for me it was almost like a lucky charm or something. And guess why I lost it." I look sideways at Silas and offer a wry smile. "It was in my blazer pocket, and I was running home after school to try and catch Silas shooting hoops in his driveway."

"Wow, seriously," Silas says as everyone else laughs at me. "I'm almost sorry I touched that thing. Or am I? Is it charmed, or cursed, lucky or unlucky?"

"None of the above, of course," Sebastian says with a chuckle. "People believe what they need to believe, like Frances said a while ago. Dumb luck. Happy coincidence. Nothing more."

"Happenstance," Mom says, smiling as she squeezes Sebastian's arm. "Something that happens by chance, with good results. A fusing of happen and circumstance. It's as if all our lives, circumstances have been spinning toward this moment in time, toward what is happening right now. Like me accidentally discovering you on Facebook after so many years. Like Tara finding the ring that Sophie lost. Silas fits into the puzzle too. And now here we all are, sitting at the counter in my home. I've always loved that word, *happenstance*. The alliteration, you know."

"Wait a sec. Accidentally discovering me on Facebook?" Sebastian says, hugging her. "You were creeping me, weren't you."

Then Mom blushes, yes actually blushes. "Is it hot in here?" she asks with a giggle.

"Get a room, you guys." Jonah smiles as he shakes his head.

A sudden, almost urgent series of knocks at the front door makes us all jump.

"Did Tara forget something?" I wonder out loud, then hurry through the hall to answer.

When I fling open the door, three women are standing there, and one of them is crying softly into her hands.

"Hi, I'm Silas's Aunt Hazel," one of them says. "This is my wife, Maggie. And this is Silas's mom, Penny Symonds."

The one who's crying. She doesn't even take her hands away from her face. Just sort of sniffles and nods her head hello. For a moment I'm speechless. This is the mother who pretty much disowned her son for being gay. And now she's crying on our doorstep. Can this day get any weirder?

"Nice to meet you all?" I say with a question in my voice. Clearly all three of them are extremely anxious about something bad that must have only just happened, and they're looking for Silas, and it's making me extremely anxious myself. I can feel my heartbeat throbbing in my throat.

"So, is Silas over here?" Hazel says, awaiting an answer as her eyes grow wider.

Sheesh, I must look like a complete bonehead right now, but I'm still frozen in shock at the sight of them.

"Oh, oh right, sorry. Yes, I'll get him. Silas, come here quick," I yell over my shoulder and then just stand there gobsmacked again. Then, "Oh, would you like to come inside?"

"What's going on," Silas says behind me, then stops dead in his tracks beside me. "Mom? Why are you here? Why are you crying? Did something happen?" There's a distinct tremor to his voice now.

"It's...it's your father," Penny sobs through her hands, then drops them slowly. "He's probably had a heart attack and he's at the hospital. And he asked to see you, Silas. Begged me to agree. And I mean, what could I say? He's hooked up to tubes and beeping monitors, and I've been so stupid about this and..."

"It's okay, Mom," Silas says as he steps forward and wraps his arms around her shoulders. And wow, she hugs him back and starts sobbing against his chest.

"I feel like it's all my fault," she murmurs. "Because I was being so stubborn. About everything, and it stressed him out so much, always said his heart hurt, and I..."

"Stop it, Mom," he says. "We can talk about all that later. You guys are coming too, right?" Silas asks Hazel and Maggie. "Can you give us a lift there? I think I need to just sit in the back seat to comfort my mom right now."

By the way his two aunts glance anxiously at each other, eyebrows raised, I can tell he's asked them something they might not be able to do right now.

"To be honest, we have tickets to see *Come From Away* at the theatre tonight," Maggie murmurs. "But look, this is far more important, and we can just let them go I guess..."

"I'll take you," I tell Silas. "I've heard those tickets are a fortune and nearly impossible to get. So, I doubt you want to miss it, right?"

"Oh thanks so much, you're a life saver," Maggie says with a smile.

"I don't know," Hazel says. "Angus is my brother. Maybe I should be there too."

Maggie wraps her arm around Hazel's shoulder.

"I'm sorry, Hazel," she says, looking sad. "I'll do whatever works best for you."

"You can't come into the ICU, anyway. Only two allowed," Penny tells them. Then she looks at me and forces a wobbly smile. "That would be wonderful. Who are you anyway?"

"Oh, I'm Sophie," I tell her. "Let me grab my mom's key and my purse."

By then Mom and Sebastian and Jonah are behind us in the hallway with looks of dismay as they watch this drama unfold. Mom grabs her key fob from the console where she dropped it and tosses it to me. I snatch my handbag up from the floor where I left it. Then I lead them to the car, leaving Hazel and Maggie at the front door with Mom, my brother, and Sebastian, to explain everything that happened.

All the way to the hospital, I can't stop thinking about the moonstone ring. Silas just had it in his hand a few minutes before his mom showed up at the door. His mom who cut off all contact and practically disowned him just because he's gay. Forced him to move in with his aunt because she couldn't handle it when he revealed his personal truth. And now clearly regrets how ridiculous it was to make such a big deal about something that isn't a big deal at all. But what a terrible way to have the sense knocked into you, like an ethical slap upside the head. The world sure works in mysterious ways. *Om mane padme hum.*

In the back seat I can hear them speaking to each other in low voices. I'm trying my best not to eavesdrop, with some indie folk rock tunes playing on Sirius XM radio. But I can still hear a little of what they're saying to each other. And the loudest word of all is 'sorry'. And it's coming from his mom, over and over again.

I'm actually starting to think that this is the best, worst thing that could have happened to their family. But deep down, I'll be really sorry if Silas decides to be super forgiving and move back home with his parents again. Even though I've just barely gotten to know him, I already feel close to him. And what's better than having a male friend with no strings attached ever. Never any awkwardness. Just a really nice guy to chill with.

The hospital is only a ten minute drive from our house. My hands are clenched on the steering wheel, as I do my best not to speed. Behind me in the back seat, it feels as if there is a breakthrough happening. As if some sort of reconciliation is taking place after so many months of overwhelming sadness. I can't stop thinking of the word 'happenstance' that my mom used. It feels like something I need to get tattooed on my arm. Everything has been spinning toward this one single moment in time. Silas and his mom reconnecting in the back seat of our car. When just a few days back I didn't even know his name.

Ever since I lost that ring, nothing has been the same, in so many connected ways.

For Silas and his mom right now, this is the *only* moment. Everything that happened before this moment doesn't even matter anymore going forward. It reminds me of everything Zen that I've been reading up on for my World Religion essay. It's so Buddhist, which is my obvious choice.

Living in the present is all that matters. Not what's coming or what's gone before. It's hard to wrap my head around thinking that way though. My mind always seems to be trapped in an endless loop of mulling everything over instead of just letting everything go and moving on. Always worrying about what everyone else is thinking instead of thinking for myself. So trapped in my own angst and worrying about all the wrong things instead of celebrating all the good things about every new second of every new day.

Om mane padme hum. I don't think there's anything harder than trying to live in the moment! Someday I may even reach a state of enlightenment if I can stay focused enough. Now that would be something to strive for.

A car horn blaring to my left snaps me out of my Buddhism-fixated trance. The hospital is right ahead. There's a place in front of the Emergency Department where I can drop them off. And that's exactly where I pull up.

"You guys can hop out here," I tell them. "I can wait if you want me to, you know. I'm not in a big hurry to be anywhere when this is so important to you."

"That's okay," Penny says in a soft voice as she places a hand on my shoulder. "You've been so helpful already. Thanks for being such a good friend to Silas."

She climbs out of the back seat, then Silas puts his hand on my shoulder too.

"This has been one of the most insane days of my life so far," he tells me in an earnest voice. He looks so much like his mom, just like Jonah and our mom. "And yes, thanks for being a new friend at the right time in the right place. It's as if you came along exactly when I needed you. Strange and random, the way things work, isn't it?"

"I've been thinking the exact same thing all the way here in the car," I admit. "Text me when you get home, or whenever you need to talk, okay."

"Be careful what you wish for," he says with a trace of a smile. And then he's gone.

And all the way home I just keep on thinking the same thing about how strange and how random the world can be. Everything just happens the way it's supposed to, I guess. Whether or not you're wearing a mysterious glimmering moonstone ring. As soon as I get home, I need to rush up to my room to add some final touches on my essay for Ms. Martino. I've had such awesome thoughts about life and the way things work, and how no matter how much you worry, nothing is going to change. Whatever happens, happens, so carpe diem. Got to write it all down now!

As I pull into the driveway and park the car, I stop for a second and take a deep breath. To try and calm down and ground myself before I go zooming inside my house again like I do every single day. Sometimes it feels as if I'm going through life at top speed, and not even paying attention to anything that's going on around me. Sometimes I honestly seem to have the attention span of a butterfly, as I flutter from one flower to another and never land anywhere for very long. And that's something else I need to try and work on.

Okay, just slow down and don't go rushing through the house like you always do, Sophie, I remind myself when I walk through the front door. Just stop and say hello to everyone, and don't be such a beeatch about being in such a hurry. I stop in the kitchen doorway where Mom and Jonah and Sebastian are sitting around an open pizza carton. The aroma is killer. I realize that I'm utterly starving.

"How did it go with Silas and his mom?" Mom asks me, looking truly concerned.

"I think this might be a turning point," I tell them. "Just the fact that she showed up here today, that she turned to Silas as soon as something terrible happened. Had second thoughts and regrets about the way she's been acting. That's huge, isn't it? And you know what? Thanks so much for being so kind and understanding about every crazy thing today, you guys."

Sebastian smiles wide. "I was happy to be here," he tells me. "I mean, it was quite a peculiar way of getting to meet everyone for the first time. But that makes it even better. I feel as if I needed to be here for this. Like it's some kind of turning point for all of us."

"I'm so glad we could help however we could, Sophie," Mom says. "We're still a family, no matter how it looks now, and we have to stick together forever."

I slip behind Mom and wrap her in a huge hug, my amazing drama queen of a matriarch.

"So, I guess you have to give up on Silas, huh," Jonah smirks through a bite of pizza.

"Well duh. Yes, it would seem so," I tell him, with a deliberate eyeroll and a shrug.

"So anyway, your new friend Tara, she's what, same age as you? Younger maybe?" Jonah says with a half frown, like he's pretending not to really care.

"A year behind me, I think. Grade ten, like you," I tell him. I raise an eyebrow as I snatch a slice of pizza and a plate from the table. "Why do you ask, brother of mine?"

"Oh, no reason," Jonah says. "Just curious. Think she'll be hanging out here now and then? She seems nice, and it looks like you guys really get along. Brand new friend. Right?"

"You can only hope," I say, then wink as, slow and deliberate, I stroll out of the room.

Chapter Eleven

Tara

As soon I leave Sophie's street, I hear a chime from my phone and stop to check my message. Because I can! Because I have a smart phone now! Another bit of luck in my recent string. The text is from Priya.

Tara THNX! U R the bff anyone ever had. So sorry for being a jerk! I O U

Uh-oh. She needs to know that she's barking up the wrong tree. She's still got it bad for Silas. She thinks something's possibly going to happen between them. She still has hope. Eesh. Should I tell her now, or just let her figure it out for herself when she kisses him for the first time and probably feels nothing, like I did. Ugh, I can't bring myself to do this right now when I'm still reeling with shock and awe over what just happened with Silas and Sophie. And when the moonstone ring is vibrating on my finger, begging me to look at it every ten seconds. So, I just text back. And hope for the best.

No worries girlfriend. Have fun with it!

Every ridiculous thing that has happened to me today feels like a slap upside the head. Just when you think you have the most screwed up family situation on the planet, you discover you're not alone. Every family is riddled with too many issues that take up way too much time and space in their lives. And then you feel stupid and selfish for even thinking that way in the first place. 'You' meaning me. Wake-up call, Tara!

So instead of texting with Priya, I head home to start packing. And to share the ring story with my mom, once and for all. Since she seems to be moving in the right direction at long last, maybe she can help me make a decision about how to get rid of it. Because this beautiful object of my affection clearly doesn't belong on my hand. Not after everything that's happened lately.

For a change she's here. Her face is rosy, her bangs damp with sweat. And she's madly packing up all the junk we've accumulated since moving here. The vintage landscape paintings she picked up cheap are gone from the walls and bundled in bubble wrap. The living room bookshelf is empty of her favourite thrillers and my childhood collection. All the knick-knacks have vanished, and every surface is bare. This thing is really happening.

"Wow, you've been busy. I won't have much left to help you with."

"You betcha, Tara. This is the most motivated I've been in absolute ages. I love it! And don't worry, your own bedroom will take up all your time. Disaster area, honey."

"You make a good point," I admit. "I've just been so busy. Got a second, Mom?"

"Sure." She blows a tendril of hair out of her eyes and perches on a box. "What's up?"

"Well, for one thing, I want to say thanks, for setting that money aside for my education. And I also want to say sorry for being so nasty lately. For not having enough faith in you. For being so judgy and rude, too."

I can't even look at her while I'm admitting these unpleasant truths. But the next moment her arms are around me and she has me trapped in a boa constrictor hug.

"Honey, I couldn't have done *any* of this without you," she says, so close to my ear that I can feel her breath. "Because no matter what's happened over the years, you've always been my voice of reason. You're the one who finally convinced me that I should ditch your dad for good. You always stuck by me and believed in me. Even when I made that bad decision to go back to him after we stayed at the shelter a few years ago. You never called me out for it. You would always just hang in there for me." She backs up and looks straight into my eyes, her hands still clutching my shoulders. "Honestly, sometimes I feel just like a flaky teenager, always making the wrong moves and dumbass decisions!"

That line squeezes a grin out of me. "Really? So do I, like, need to give you a curfew, with this new love interest in your life?"

Mom starts giggling like a dumb teenager. "Isn't Dave the best," she says. "He just has this way of making me feel so good about myself. And I haven't laughed so much in...ever."

"I'm glad, Mom. So far so good. And I actually like this guy." Then I dig into my pocket and pull it out. "So, this ring I found last Friday? It's the real deal. And you will not even believe the story that goes along with it, and the new friends and questionable decisions I've made just since the day that I found it."

Her eyes grow wide. "Aha! I thought that looked expensive. Somebody out there must be so upset about losing it. But why haven't you turned it into the police yet?"

"Let's make a pot of Earl Grey. Because I've got quite the little story to share."

My mom listens quietly the entire time. She rolls her eyes when I explain about the supposed special powers of the moonstone. How I'd almost felt super-charged wearing it.

"Powers, huh? If there's one lesson I've learned over the years," she says. "It's that people can talk themselves into believing almost anything. The power of suggestion is extremely strong. And trust me, Tara, you've had those powers, that inner strength, from the start."

Hmm. Sometimes that mom of mine can make some pretty good points. She leans in closer when I start to tell her about Sophie and Silas, and what they've each been through with their own families. Her eyes even well up with tears at one point as she nods knowingly.

"Sophie says it was 'sheer dumb luck' when she lost the ring," I explain, staring at the milky stone. "What does that even mean? What's so dumb about it?"

"It's just a saying." Mom plucks the ring from my hand and studies it closely. "Dumb luck is when something good happens, completely by chance."

"Sort of like happenstance?" I say.

"Yeah," Mom says. "That's the perfect word for it."

"Cool. Well, I know I can't keep this," I murmur, still staring at those two twinkling diamonds. "I know that my time with this ring is pretty much up. What was the name of that shelter that we stayed at? I can't even remember anymore. All I know is that I felt safe there."

"Helena's Haven. Named after the woman who started it," Mom says. "And the fact is, most women's shelters rely on donations." She offers me the gentlest of smiles. I've almost forgotten how pretty my mom can be. "I think I see where you're going with this, Tara Bear."

"I think I finally do too," I tell her.

That evening when Mom and Dave and I drop the ring off at Helena's Haven, they are blown away. They admire the exquisiteness of that unique and mystical piece of jewelry. And they can't decide whether to sell it on eBay or hold a silent auction as a fundraiser.

I know it will be good karma whichever route they choose. I omitted the history of the moonstone ring, just told the shelter administrator when she asked, that it wound up in my hands by sheer dumb luck. She told me they were the lucky ones today. And I was more than happy to leave it behind and move on to more pressing problems.

* * *

I don't meet Silas face to face all day Wednesday, and he never shows up in the cafeteria at lunch time. Even though we seemed to have made a breakthrough around Sophie's counter, I get the feeling he's still trying to avoid me. And every time I catch a glimpse of him in the hallways, he's mostly alone, and he seems lost in thought and completely distracted. I wonder what's going on with him. But I'm afraid to ask in case it's about me.

Then, much later that night, after that very weird week, I have the strangest dream. Sophie and I are strolling alongside each other on the sidewalk where I first found the ring and everything started to change. Only this time it's dark, except for a full moon that looks like a slice of potato, hanging ripe and low in the night sky, and a spattering of diamond stars.

Even though it's pitch dark, we both spot the sparkling ring at the exact same moment. It seems to be almost glowing, as if it's being super-charged by moonlight. We both reach for it at the exact same instant. We touch it together, and I feel a tingling in my fingertips. Sophie looks at me and smiles, wide-eyed. She's felt it too. Then suddenly, poof, the ring seems to dissolve before our eyes. Sophie and I gaze at each other with something like wonderment and understanding. We link arms. And we keep on walking toward that ever-gleaming moon.

When I awaken with a start, and glance at my clock, it's 3:00 a.m. I still feel as if I'm glowing from the inside out. And I fall back to sleep with a smile on my face.

The next morning, when I turn on my phone and check it first thing, as usual these days, a text message from Sophie pops up very first thing. (Because yes, we exchanged numbers. I have an actual new friend!) So bizarre after that dream last night. Her message is even weirder.

I just had the strangest dream about you. Must be the ring. Lol
Sent at 3:01 a.m.

Hmm. I wonder if she had the same...nah. Not even possible. But whatever! Nice to hear from her at least. I text her right back.

* * *

By Friday I've pretty much given up hope on running into Silas. I know he still isn't happy that I'm missing important rehearsals, and he's clearly too nice to call me out on it. So, I guess it's way easier for him to not even face me at all. Besides, his role in the play is super important to him, so I'm giving him the benefit of the doubt this time because he must be totally focused on it with the first dress rehearsal this Saturday. Priya is still madly enthusiastic about the play. I'm so glad I found a simple way to mend our friendship by giving her this opportunity to play a big part for a few days. And be close to the most popular guy in the production of *Our Town*.

Even though I left out the most critical information of all. Hope she won't be too mad at me when she finds out, which is inevitable eventually.

"Silas and I are really starting to connect on stage. We're melting right into our roles. When he looks into my eyes, I feel like Emily," she tells me at lunch time Friday. "So, if you suddenly happen to get sick or something, then I can definitely fill in for you.”

“Well, that’s great to hear,” I say, swallowing hard.

Then immediately start to doubt myself. What if she truly is way better than me as Emily Webb? What if Ms. Wilding decides she should replace me with Priya for the entire production? What if I’ve made the biggest mistake of my life by giving her a few days in the limelight?

I chew my lip, and focus on my salami and cheese sandwich. Then tell Priya about meeting Sophie, and giving up the ring to Helena’s Haven, and even the lottery win, just to change the subject. She says she’s proud of me, thrilled that everything is going so well for Mom and me now. I smile, nod, try to pretend I’m not totally freaked out by everything else she just told me.

After school, I can’t resist showing up in the auditorium. I miss the thrill of being on stage. Besides, my room is all packed up. Dave helped us start moving our things into the new place the last couple of nights and we’re sleeping there for the first time tonight. It’s definitely tiny. But it’s renovated, with shining stainless steel appliances, refinished hardwood floors, and an updated kitchen, maple cupboards with doors on them that actually stay shut. The toilet even flushes properly, no plunger necessary. Yes, Mom and I are definitely moving up in the world.

I sneak in after the cast is assembled on stage and sit in the back row, trying to decide if I should stick around for the whole thing. How will it affect me to watch Silas and Priya feeling so 'comfortable' together? When the Stage Manager character steps forward and begins the opening lines of the play, my heart starts to pick up speed. When Priya recites her very first lines as Emily, I slide down in my seat until just the top of my head is showing. Their first scene together is coming up soon. How can I possibly handle this?

And then there they are, together at centre stage, talking about communicating with each other through their bedroom windows and giving each other 'hints', almost in a flirty way. And—I cannot believe it—they are utterly awful. Almost hard to watch, awkward and wooden. Silas doesn't look comfortable at all. Ms. Wilding makes them start the scene over three times before she lets them carry on, and it still doesn't turn out well. It makes me feel all prickly inside out. I slip away at the end of Act I because I just can't bear to watch them anymore.

* * *

When my cell phone rings just before our very first dinner in our new home that evening, just the two of us because lovely Dave said so, Mom grins at me.

"You're liking that phone, aren't you," she says as she dumps pasta into boiling water.

"Yup. Digging the high-tech life now," I tell her. Then I check call display. Priya?

"Hey, what's up," I ask. Silence. "Priya? What's going on?"

A huge sniffle followed by a muffled sob.

"I suck as Emily Webb," she murmurs. "I absolutely suck. Silas is freaking out. Tara, I just can't do this anymore. You have to come back tomorrow, for our dress rehearsal."

"Oh no, Priya. What happened? You said you guys are comfortable on stage."

"We have no chemistry, Silas and me. We're like a couple of robots. Ugh, and when we have to kiss I just feel so nervous and weird, like we're not even connecting. So, it makes me feel as if he doesn't even like being on stage with me. Everybody can tell. Ms. Wilding is totally frustrated so we have to keep on starting our scenes over. She's losing patience." Priya sniffles some more.

"I don't know what to say." I know what I need to say though. And now is the perfect time to tell her the truth. Now that she's felt it the same way that I did when I had to kiss Silas in the wedding scene. The zero zap of a kiss that means nothing. "Okay maybe I do. There's something you need to know, Priya, so that you can just move forward, and leave all this behind." I take a deep breath.

"Oh no," she murmurs. "You two are going out already. And you hid it from me. That's why the kiss meant nothing, like he wasn't even trying. I knew I shouldn't have left Starbucks on Saturday night."

Oh brother. Talk about overthinking things. And I thought I was bad.

"Not even close. So, guess what. Silas is...well, he's gay, Priya. There, now you know."

"Silas is *gay*? The new guy you keep talking about who plays George? I got the feeling you were crushing on him," Mom whispers. I nod and shrug and put a finger to my lips.

"Well how about that," she says, grinning as she spoons pasta sauce onto our bowls.

And then, after too long a pause, I hear a drawn-out sigh from my friend.

"Whew. OMG I thought it was just me. When I felt nothing during that awkward brief kiss, and just couldn't fake feel it like I should, you know, to make it believable as an actor. But it's not just that. We have zero stage chemistry. I'm too new at this, and I can't do it anymore because it doesn't feel right. Just...just say you'll come back."

"Say I'll come back?" Priya actually sees the problems. She doesn't want to be on stage with Silas. And I didn't even have to tell her myself. She figured it all out on her own. It feels as if a huge weight has just lifted off my chest. In fact, so much that's been weighing down my spirits lately has changed for the better. And I'm feeling lighter than I have in ages. Almost free.

"Please Tara. Just come to dress rehearsal tomorrow morning, okay? Everyone will be thrilled if you step back into the Emily Webb role right away. Especially George Gibbs. Hah, I mean Silas. Trust me. Every day he asks me when you'll be coming back."

Silas wants me back? What utterly awesome news. I am going to slay the Emily role!

"Seriously?" A little flame starts to flicker inside me. I will nail that role with him.

"Totally! Because I can't do this anymore. I guess I wasn't meant for being on stage." I can hear her blowing her nose. "And you have to promise not to get sick, because I'll die of embarrassment if I have to fake kiss Silas one more time."

Oh yay! Can't let on how relieved and pumped I am. Don't want to hurt her feelings. Big fake sigh required.

"Well, only if you're sure, Priya. And I guess it should be okay with my mom, since we're pretty much all moved in now. I'll see you at dress rehearsal tomorrow, then."

"Oh thanks so much," Priya says. "You are, you realize, the absolute BFF ever."

"Ditto Priya," I tell her before ending the call.

'Oh, earth, you're too wonderful for anybody to realize you.'

That Emily Webb line echoing in my head is the truth. More than I've ever realized myself until this moment. I should never take things for granted, like the possibility that people can never change. Mom has grown so much, and I've only just started to appreciate that, finally. And not everything is always awful either. Even though it might feel that way sometimes. That hopeful thought makes me smile wider than I have in absolute ages. I think I might almost be starting to like my life. That shiny makeover might actually be happening.

When I hang up, my lovely mom is staring at me. "Everything okay, honey?" she asks.

"Yup, it most truly is almost *too* wonderful now, Mom."

* * *

Then later that evening, when I'm alone in my new bedroom going over and over my lines after texting Silas that I'm back in the role, he finally responds.

Sorry Tara, I was just out on Sophie's front porch talking. Like almost every night now lol! I'm so-o-o-o-o-o-o glad ur coming back tomorrow. Whew. Poor Priya was so nervous. She couldn't pull it off. But you will nail the Emily Webb role.

OMG Silas thanx for saying that!!!

I said it cuz it's true! So guess what. My dad had to go to the hospital and get his heart checked Tuesday. He will be fine tho. But ever since it happened, Mom and I are fine now too! It was like a wake-up call for her. It's gonna be ok with us from now on.

What what what!!! Yay yay yay!!! This is the best news ever.

Totally. Now go work on your lines lol

Hah! Me??? You too dude. Seeya tmrw!!!

When I catch a glimpse of myself in my dresser mirror, I'm almost surprised to catch myself smiling. But it's hard not to smile today after everything that's happened in my life lately. I almost have to pinch myself because of everything I have to be grateful for now. Silas Symonds is awesome. And no wonder he was so preoccupied all week. I'm so happy for his family. Sophie is lucky she lives next door to someone as cool as that guy. Even though the bouncing basketball is driving her nuts. I hope we have cool neighbours here in our new house too.

I so wish I could hang out with Sophie sometimes. I was really getting to like her during this whole ring thing, like we became moonstone sisters or something. Even though that sounds a bit weird and needy. Fingers crossed we'll stay friends. I haven't even told her what I did with the ring yet. I hope she and her mom both approve. And I also desperately hope that she reaches out at some point, but I don't want to keep on bugging her and actually sounding desperate. Especially since she's a year ahead of me. Oh, and her brother, Jonah. Crazy cute.

Okay, enough daydreaming Tara. Like Silas said, go work on your lines so you can prove yourself on stage during dress rehearsal tomorrow morning. You need to put your heart and soul into it. You need to blow away the entire cast and crew this time. Because like Silas also said, you're going to nail the Emily Webb role.

Not half an hour later, though, my phone chimes and the screen lights up. And yay, it's a message from Sophie! Along with a photo.

From Silas lol

When I click on the photo, I laugh out loud, and text right back.

Lol awesome! He finally figured it out!

And in this exact moment in time, I almost feel too wonderful for words just thinking about everything that's going to happen next.

* * *

Sophie

Later on Tuesday, just when I'm hunkered down at my desk, putting the finishing touches on my essay, the bouncing starts again. And I'm not sure whether to feel ecstatic or annoyed. But Silas is home already, so that must be a very good thing, since I only just dropped them off at the hospital ER. Didn't I?

I check my muted phone, which I left across the room, plugged in and charging. Yikes, it's getting on to 8:30. I've been working for nearly three hours and making great progress. But what have I missed? A ton of text messages and missed calls from Lexi and some of our other friends. Ugh, it's just so draining, all this drama. I've had enough for one day, and I don't feel like getting caught up in the latest stupid plights of my too-needy friends. So instead, I decide to take a break from my desk and head outside to talk to Silas. Find out how it went at the hospital with his dad and mom and their whole reconciliation thing.

Jonah's bedroom door is shut which means he must be studying. And there's nobody on the main floor as I head for the front door, which means Mom is probably off somewhere with Sebastian. I think they might have mentioned heading out to see a movie when I popped down for a second slice of pizza a couple of hours ago.

Tonight is unusually warm for an April evening. And there's a wide pearly slice of moon smiling down from the twilit sky. Which immediately reminds me of the moonstone ring. I feel a surge of relief that it's gone now from our lives. And that Mom is finally moving on at long last.

"Hey, Silas," I call out over the bouncing sound, as I settle into one of the chairs on our front porch. "I'm almost afraid to ask, but how did it go?"

The bouncing stops right away.

"Hey, you," Silas calls back as he strides over to the porch. "My plan worked. I figured you might wander out here when you heard my bouncing. Knew you were working on that essay, so I didn't want to text you, make you feel obligated to come out and talk."

"So, guess what," I tell him. "It's time to be honest. The bouncing is making me a bit crazy. I can't work when it's happening. Like a jackhammer in my brain."

"What!" he gasps. "You should have said something sooner. I don't have to be doing this all the time, you know."

"But it helps you concentrate and stay focused," I remind him. "As you told me."

"Yeah, but that doesn't work for you. So, I can stop. I mean, if it bugs you too much."

Wow, Silas is being way too nice about this. Other people wouldn't even give a crap!

"Look, we can find a compromise," I tell him. "Like, let's say, a set of noise cancelling headphones. I just need to order some online or something. No worries."

"You sure?" he says. "Well maybe, but from now on I'll just text you first, and make sure you're not working on something important."

"We're going in circles," I tell him. "So just chill. It's not a big deal. We'll figure out a plan that works for both of us. Just tell me what happened at the hospital before I scream!"

"Wow, dramatic like your mom, huh," he says with a bit of a snicker. "You will not believe what happened in the ER. My dad isn't even in the ICU yet. Mom was all panicky and confused. He's still waiting for tests to happen and hooked up to monitors. Mom let me go in alone so that I could talk to him. And..." His lips curl into a half smile as he shakes his head.

"And...and...spill it will you!"

"Well, you know how your mom let on that your housekeeper Dhanu gave her the ring, when she actually swiped it for spite?"

"Yeah, but what has this got to do with...no! Seriously?"

"Pretty much, I think."

"You mean your dad's actually FAKING it?"

Silas shrugs. "I can't be absolutely certain. But he did say something weird when I asked him how he was feeling, first thing. He said 'I'm feeling so much better now, Silas. Hopefully this might even be a false alarm. Like a wakeup call.' And then, well, I think he might have winked!"

"Wow, come on. That's insane!"

"Maybe, maybe not," Silas says with a sigh. "He was heartbroken over this mess. So, I figure maybe it really did have an effect on his heart. I googled it, you know, and it's an actual thing. Heartbreak can cause all kinds of physical symptoms. And in the car on the way, Mom said he'd been complaining of chest pains lately. My dad and I are super close. He used to shoot hoops with me in our driveway. All the time. We've been going on camping trips with my cousins since I was small. And I'm an only child. This six-month fallout was killing him."

"And what about your mom? Did you guys resolve anything? You were having a real heart to heart in the back seat, no pun intended. She sounded devastated, from what I could hear. Will things change now?"

"They already have. She promised she would never judge me again. And admitted how much she missed me but was too stubborn to change her mind. Plus, the pressure from her hard-ass intolerant family. I heard her on the phone with my grandfather. And she basically told him to eff off in so many words. I felt proud of her, for the first time in almost forever."

This is the best news for Silas and his sad situation. And the worst news for me.

"So does that mean..." I swallow hard. "Does that mean you're moving back home now, Silas? I mean, I understand why you would, of course, but...wow I can't believe

I'm being so selfish. But I'll miss you so much, and I've hardly just met you."

Silas sidles right over to my chair and wraps me in a strong warm hug.

"Relax," he says. "No decisions being made yet. But here's the thing. I really like my new school. Better than my old one. And they have a great drama club here too. So, I figure my folks and I will make a compromise. I'll finish up the rest of this year and next at Cedarvale, instead of going back to my old high school. I'll live here during the week, and at home on weekends. Home for the summer, too. So, it's sort of like I'm living in residence, right?"

"You've really thought this through," I tell him. His face is so close to mine for a second before he plops down in one of our porch chairs. I've already gotten to love that face, those dark sweet coffee-coloured eyes. "At least I get to have you here part of the time. So yay for that!"

"Right?" Wicked grin. "As well as the dreaded bouncing basketball. But think of all the schoolwork you can get done on weekends when you don't have to listen to that sound."

"I'd rather have you here," I admit. "I love knowing you're nearby to talk sometimes."

"We can text anytime though. I can even meet you at Starbucks sometimes," he says.

"So, are you actually asking me on a date, dude? Be still my happy heart!"

When I offer my own wicked grin, we both crack up.

Silas and I make plans. We get stuff figured out. We're friends now, and we will stay friends. He fills me in on the schedule for the *Our Town* production at Cedarvale. I plan on going to at least half of the productions, and hopefully hanging out with some of the cast afterwards. After all, I have a couple of new friends in the lead roles. Tara and I have been texting. I'm getting to like her more and more. But if Jonah asks when she's coming over again, I might just blow a gasket. Actually, Tara has asked about my sweet weirdo of a brother a lot, too. Hmm. Maybe she's trying to get to him through me?

Oh, who even cares! *Om mane padme hum.* Somehow or other, I know we're both moonstone spirits, Tara and I, linked forever by a maybe mysterious ring. Okay, enough dwelling on everything, Sophie.

'Be where you are; otherwise you will miss your life.'

Buddha said that, apparently, and the thought won't leave my head. Maybe it should be a new way of thinking for me. Sometimes mindfulness feels impossible, but it's so worth a shot!

* * *

On Wednesday night, after my first day at school without Lexi in probably my entire life, a day with zero angst for a change, I have the strangest dream.

I'm walking along the same sidewalk where I get off the bus every day, in pretty much the same place where I lost the ring. Someone is walking beside me, and when I look over, I realize that it's Tara. Only instead of sunshine, it's pitch dark. Above us, ahead of us, the moon has risen, like a moonstone ghost, actually. With scattered stars glittering all around like diamonds on black velvet.

Then, at the same instant, we spot it. The moonstone ring, just lying there, waiting to be found. It's all lit up in an eerie way, as if it's siphoning light and power from the moon. Tara and I both reach for the ring at the exact same instant. Together we touch it, and together, I know by the surprised look on her face, we each feel a sudden tingling sensation. Tara looks at me, wide-eyed and smiling and I smile back. And then suddenly, poof, the ring just dissolves into nothingness. Gone in a flash, just like that.

And that's when we gaze at each other for a second, gobsmacked, then link arms and keep right on walking in the direction of the moonlit sky and scintillating stars.

I sit up with a gasp and look at the clock. 3:00 a.m. I probably shouldn't text her right now, in case her phone is turned on and wakes her up, but I do anyway.

I just had the strangest dream about you. Must be the ring. Lol

I fall back asleep feeling strangely happy for the first time in practically forever. The next morning when I check my phone, there's a text message from Tara.

Lol me too! Bizarre huh!

* * *

The rest of the week is strange indeed, without Lexi and her neediness sucking up everyone's time and energy. It's such a nice change. I'm sure Lexi doesn't understand why I never responded to all her messages back on Tuesday when everything crazy was happening all at once. Or why I haven't come to the rescue to help her dream up some solutions to all her latest dilemmas when she calls and texts.

She has to stay home from school for a couple of weeks, which went into effect right after that meeting with the principal. And most evenings this week I've been heading outside to talk to Silas as soon as the bouncing starts after dinner. It's become a thing now. More than ever, I've been bouncing the basketball myself. And I'm actually better at getting the ball through the hoop now, too.

Friday evening when I'm watching a Netflix movie in my room, there's suddenly a whole bunch of action on my phone, along with a new string of text messages. It's been so great to take a break from Lexi and always having our agenda planned. And I'm totally enjoying this rare Friday evening home. Most of the urgent SOS texts are from Lexi, who is clearly losing it. And needs to share her angst, of course.

SOS need u guys right now
Meeting at starbucks SOS
Be there or you're done for SOS

And then an actual pissed-off selfie in Starbucks, giving us all the finger. Wow.

After that a whole series of chirps and calls from the rest of the girls. Asking where I am and why I'm not answering Lexi. Telling me that I need to get over to Starbucks right away. They are there right now, and Lexi is crying her eyes out. She found out she's grounded Saturdays until the end of the school year. And she has to spend the entire summer at their family cottage, will be forced to get a summer job up there. Instead of staying home with the housekeeper the way she usually does and doing mostly nothing at all besides post on social media and shop online. Oh, and drive all her friends crazy too, of course.

Poor suffering Lexi. How will she ever survive this utterly traumatic experience that's destroying her life. I guess I should start with texting Lexi first, since she's the one who apparently needs help big time SOS.

What's up Lex?

Where r u!!!!! I need u right now! U missed my SOS!

I was watching a movie.

Why did you ignore me all week? U never call back.

School work. Plus, I was busy outside a lot. Talking to Silas. He's been dealing with some nasty stuff. But things are getting better for him now. so yay for that!

What? But I have nasty stuff too. And U hardly no him.

His was way worse than yours. Trust me.

Nobodys is worse than mine. Did he get suspended?

U need to get a grip Lex.

Well did he? Come to starbucks. We're having a meeting. Need u hear.

That doesn't work for me right now.

What!!!!! Please Soph.

Take a deep breath. Om mane padme hum. Get yourself grounded.

WTF! what does that even mean? And I AM grounded.

JFGI. Just fucking google it. lol

Your being such a bitch.

Am I? And learn to spell lol.

Your scaring me. Stop it Sophie.

Okay. Over and out.

What is wrong with u. why r u doing this to me.

Hello? Answer me.

Please come over here I need u RITE NOW!

Wow, this girl is utterly exhausting and drains my brain even more than that bouncing basketball next door. This has become even more clear over the last few days since I lost that ring and found some new friends. Some bizarre sort of happenstance that threw us all together. It's almost as if the moonstone ring played a part in shining a light on my life. And helping me to look outside myself and see what's really going on.

I realize that Lexi will always be a part of my life one way or another. But I also realize that I don't need to answer to her every whim. She needs to fend for herself. She's more than a bit mixed up, but maybe she'll actually learn something from everything that just happened. I can only hope, I guess.

Every family and every friendship looks so different. It's really just dumb luck, whichever you happen to land in the instant you burst into the world and begin your life story. And in so many ways we all have the same sort of problems cluttering up our life stories. The solutions are out there waiting to be found. If we're willing to look and listen. Note to self: from now on, look and listen before you judge anyone. As much as Dhanu was wrong about so many things, she was right about how you can never know what's going on in anyone else's life. Maybe someday when this is all behind us, I might even find a way to forgive her. And my dad as well.

When my phone vibrates, I shudder for a second in case it's Lexi chirping me again. But when I check, it's a text from Silas. I love having him living next door, and I also love chilling on my front steps and his, like we've been doing every evening this week.

Sophie. Go check the chair on your front porch.

Hmm. Interesting. Must investigate.

I waste no time racing from my bedroom, down the steps and out the door. I spot it right away. A set of noise cancelling headphones.

Amazing! Where did u get these?

Found out Hazel has a set she never uses. Use them til u get yours.

U r the best. Hey. Want to go to starbucks for a while?

So r u actually asking me on a date, dude? Lol sure. Be right out.

Sweet. He cracks me up. I take a photo of the headphones and text it to Tara.

From Silas lol.

Lol awesome! He finally figured it out!

Hey, we're going to Starbucks. Want to meet us there?

Cool! I was just practicing my lines. Need a break. Already OMW Sophie! Wait til u hear what I did with the ring!

Really? Well wait til you hear what I did with the reward money

Yay! Hmm. So do you think Jonah wants to go out for a while too???

Maybe…

"Hey, Jonah, want to come to Starbucks with me and Silas and Tara?" I yell upstairs.

"Yuuup!" he yells back.

Within seconds he's beside me at the front door. Tara will be thrilled.

"Thought you'd never ask," he says with a sheepish smile that melts my heart. He already seems to be feeling better after so many hard issues are starting to get resolved.

A couple of seconds later, Silas joins us out there rocking a super-wide grin. All week he's been almost glowing from the inside out now that his family has reunited. I truly am so fortunate in so many ways to suddenly have all these awesome people filling up my life. So is it fate, or is it luck, that picks your people for you, I wonder.

Maybe, just maybe, it's a little bit of both.

The End

Debra Loughead is the author of more than 40 books for children and young adults. She has conducted workshops and held readings at schools, festivals and conferences across the country. She has also written and directed children's plays, and taught creative writing classes for adults in Toronto. Debra's books have been translated into seven languages, and her award-winning poetry and adult fiction have appeared in a variety of Canadian publications.

Debra lives with her husband Dan in Toronto and Gravenhurst, Ontario. Her three adult sons have long flown the coop.